G000081035

J.Poole - Special Agent of the SCP Foundation

Case Files

1-3

Addendum files included

J. Poole : Agent of the Foundation

J.Poole - Special Agent for the SCP Foundation

AMAZON PUBLISHING
www.AMAZON.com

Published by Amazon.com

Dedication

To my cats, Crazy Furry Beasts

To my wife, Crazy Beautiful Lady

Acknowledgments

ABOUT THE AUTHOR

Steven Luther Stamm is a writer, philosopher, IT department head, Essayist, Semiotician, cook, volunteer worker and certified intercultural communications specialist.

He studied at Freed-Hardeman university and earned a bachelors degree in Public Relations with a focus on intercultural communications. Pursuing this Mr.Stamm then used the Harvardx program online to gain a associates degree in IT management. As well as completing courses of study in intercultural communications (becoming a highly educated intercultural liason) and social media management.

As of 2020 Mr. Stamm has also pursued and completed a micro masters in business administration through Harvardx. Earning him a MMBA. Mr.Stamm is also the current leading member of his local chapter of the Transhumanist party.

He is married to his wife Jana Stamm, and lives in a small duplex as he follows his full masters degree through online courses offered by the University of Tartu (through their EDX and online offerings).

J. Poole : Agent of the Foundation

Also by Steven L. Stamm

Tobias Schmit : Auditor for the supernatural

Hobbes 2020 : bringing contractulisim into the 21st century

J. Poole : Agent of the Foundation
INTRODUCTION

"A Brief overview of the world of the foundation"

===

A letter from the administrator,

Mankind in its present state has been around for a quarter of a million years, yet only the last 4,000 have been of any significance.

So, what did we do for nearly 250,000 years? We huddled in caves and around small fires, fearful of the things that we didn't understand. It was more than explaining why the sun came up, it was the mystery of enormous birds with heads of men and rocks that came to life. So we called them 'gods' and 'demons', begged them to spare us, and prayed for salvation.

In time, their numbers dwindled and ours rose. The world began to make more sense when there were fewer things to fear, yet the unexplained can never truly go away, as if the universe demands the absurd and impossible.

Mankind must not go back to hiding in fear. No one else will protect us, and we must stand up for ourselves.

While the rest of mankind dwells in the light, we must stand in the darkness to fight it, contain it, and shield it from the eyes of the public, so that others may live in a sane and normal world.

-The Administrator

MISSION STATEMENT

Operating clandestine and worldwide, the Foundation operates beyond jurisdiction, empowered and entrusted by every major national government with the task of containing anomalous objects, entities, and phenomena. These anomalies pose a significant threat to global security by threatening either physical or psychological harm.

The Foundation operates to maintain normalcy, so that the worldwide civilian population can live and go on with their daily lives without fear, mistrust, or doubt in their personal beliefs, and to maintain human independence from extraterrestrial, extradimensional, and other extranormal influence.
Our mission is three-fold:

Secure
The Foundation secures anomalies with the goal of preventing them from falling into the hands of civilian or rival agencies, through extensive observation and surveillance and by acting to intercept such anomalies at the earliest opportunity.

Contain
The Foundation contains anomalies with the goal of preventing their influence or effects from spreading, by either relocating, concealing, or dismantling such anomalies or by suppressing or preventing public dissemination of knowledge thereof.

Protect
The Foundation protects humanity from the effects of such anomalies as well as the anomalies themselves until such time that they are either fully understood or new theories of science can be devised based on their properties and behavior. The Foundation may also neutralize or destroy anomalies as an option of last resort, if they are determined to be too dangerous to be contained.
Foundation Operations
Foundation covert and clandestine operations are undertaken across the globe in pursuit of our primary missions.
Special Containment Procedures

The Foundation maintains an extensive database of information regarding anomalies requiring Special Containment

Procedures, commonly referred to as "SCPs". The primary Foundation database contains summaries of such anomalies and emergency procedures for maintaining or re-establishing safe containment in the case of a containment breach or other event.

Anomalies may take many forms, be it an object, an entity, a location, or a free-standing phenomenon. These anomalies are categorized into one of several Object Classes and are either contained at one of the Foundation's myriad Secure Facilities or contained on-site if relocation is deemed unfeasible.

Operational Security

The Foundation operates with the utmost secrecy. All Foundation personnel must observe the Security Clearance Levels as well as need-to-know and compartmentalization of information. Personnel found in violation of Foundation security protocols will be identified, detained, and subject to disciplinary action.

OBJECT CLASSES

All anomalous objects, entities, and phenomena requiring Special Containment Procedures are assigned an Object Class. An Object Class is a part of the standard SCP template and serves as a rough indicator for how difficult an object is to contain. In universe, Object Classes are for the purposes of identifying containment needs, research priority, budgeting, and other considerations. An SCP's Object Class is determined by a number of factors, but the most important factors are the difficulty and the purpose of its containment.

Primary Classes

Safe

Safe-class SCPs are anomalies that are easily and safely contained. This is often due to the fact that the Foundation has researched the SCP well enough that containment does not require significant resources or that the anomalies require a specific and conscious activation or trigger. Classifying an SCP as Safe, however, does not mean that handling or activating it does not pose a threat.

Euclid

Euclid-class SCPs are anomalies that require more resources to contain completely or where containment isn't always reliable. Usually this is because the SCP is insufficiently understood or inherently unpredictable. Euclid is the Object Class with the greatest scope, and it's usually a safe bet that an SCP will be this class if it doesn't easily fall into any of the other standard Object Classes.

Keter

Keter-class SCPs are anomalies that are exceedingly difficult to contain consistently or reliably, with containment procedures often being extensive and complex. The Foundation often can't contain these SCPs well due to not having a solid understanding of the anomaly, or lacking the technology to properly contain or counter it. A Keter SCP does not mean the SCP is dangerous, just that it is simply very difficult or costly to contain.

Thaumiel

Thaumiel-class SCPs are anomalies that the Foundation specifically uses to contain other SCPs. Even the mere existence of Thaumiel-class objects is classified at the highest levels of the Foundation and their locations, functions, and current status are known to few Foundation personnel outside of the O5 Council.

Object Class FAQ
What is the Locked Box Test?
The Locked Box Test is an informal guideline used to

determine an object's most appropriate Object Class. It goes like this:

If you lock it in a box, leave it alone, and nothing bad will happen, then it's probably Safe.

If you lock it in a box, leave it alone, and you're not entirely sure what will happen, then it's probably Euclid.

If you lock it in a box, leave it alone, and it easily escapes, then it's probably Keter.

If it is the box, then it's probably Thaumiel.

Note that as a special consideration, something that is autonomous, alive, and/or sapient is almost always at least Euclid-class. That is, if you lock a living thing in a box and forget about it, it will eventually suffocate or starve to death, and that's not a good outcome. Something that is intelligent could also end up being smart enough to outwit its containment procedures and/or stop cooperating with the Foundation's attempts to contain it, making it more dangerous than it otherwise might be.

Security Clearance Levels

Foundation security clearances granted to personnel represent the highest level or type of information to which they can be granted access. However, having any given clearance level does not automatically grant access to all information at that level: personnel are only granted access to information on a "need-to-know" basis and at the discretion of the designated disclosure officer overseeing their respective departments.

LEVEL 0 (FOR OFFICIAL USE ONLY)
Level 0 security clearances are given to non-essential personnel with no need to access information regarding anomalous objects or entities in Foundation containment. Level 0 access is typically held by personnel in non-secured clerical, logistics, or janitorial positions at facilities with no access to

operational data.

LEVEL 1 (CONFIDENTIAL)
Level 1 security clearances are given to personnel working in proximity to but with no direct, indirect, or informational access to anomalous objects or entities in containment. Level 1 security clearances are typically granted to personnel working in clerical, logistics, or janitorial positions at facilities with containment capability or otherwise must handle sensitive information.

LEVEL 2 (RESTRICTED)
Level 2 security clearances are given to security and research personnel that require direct access to information regarding anomalous objects and entities in containment. Most research staff, field agents, and containment specialists hold a Level 2 security clearance.

LEVEL 3 (SECRET)
Level 3 security clearances are given to senior security and research personnel that require in-depth data regarding the source, recovery circumstances, and long-term planning for anomalous objects and entities in containment. Most senior research staff, project managers, security officers, response team members, and Mobile Task Force operatives hold a Level 3 security clearance.

LEVEL 4 (TOP SECRET)
Level 4 security clearances are given to senior administration that require access to site-wide and/or regional intelligence as well as long-term strategic data regarding Foundation operations and research projects. Level 4 security clearances are typically only held by Site Directors, Security Directors, or Mobile Task Force Commanders.

LEVEL 5 (THAUMIEL)

Level 5 security clearances are given to the highest-ranking administrative personnel within the Foundation and grant effectively unlimited access to all strategic and otherwise sensitive data. Level 5 security clearances are typically only granted to O5 Council members and selected staff.

STAFF TITLES
THESE ARE GENERAL OCCUPATIONAL TITLES THAT ARE TYPICALLY USED IN THE FOUNDATION.

Site Staff

CONTAINMENT SPECIALIST
Containment specialists have two main roles at Foundation facilities. Firstly, containment teams are called upon to respond to confirmed cases of anomalous activity to secure and establish initial containment over anomalous objects, entities, or phenomena and transport them to the nearest Foundation containment site. In addition, Foundation containment engineers and technicians are called upon to devise, refine, and maintain containment units and schemes for objects, entities, and phenomena in Foundation facilities.

RESEARCHER
Researchers are the scientific branch of the Foundation, drawn from the ranks of the smartest and best-trained research scientists from around the world. With specialists in every field imaginable, from chemistry and botany to more esoteric or specialized fields such as theoretical physics and xenobiology, the goal of the Foundation's research projects is to gain a better understanding of unexplained anomalies and how they operate.
Security Officer

ON-SITE SECURITY OFFICERS
— often referred to simply as guards —

at Foundation facilities are tasked with maintaining physical and information security for Foundation projects, operations, and personnel. Primarily drawn and recruited from military, law enforcement, and correctional facility personnel, security officers are trained in the use of all types of weapons as well as a variety of contingency plans covering both containment breach incidents as well as hostile action. These personnel are also responsible for information security, such as making sure that sensitive documents are not misplaced and that a facility's computer systems are safe from outside intrusion. They are also often the first line of defense against hostile outside forces for Foundation facilities.

TACTICAL RESPONSE OFFICER
Response teams — or tactical teams — are highly trained and heavily armed combat teams tasked with escorting containment teams when dangerous anomalous entities or hostile Groups of Interest are involved and defending Foundation facilities against hostile action. Response teams are effectively military units stationed at major Foundation facilities that are ready to deploy at a moment's notice.

Field Personnel

FIELD AGENT
Field agents are the eyes and ears of the Foundation, personnel trained to look for and investigate signs of anomalous activity, often undercover with local or regional law enforcement or embedded in local services such as emergency medical services and regulatory organizations. As undercover units, field agents are typically not equipped to deal with confirmed cases of anomalous activity; once such an incident has been confirmed and isolated, field agents will typically call for assistance from the nearest field containment team with the means to safely secure and contain such anomalies.

MOBILE TASK FORCE OPERATIVE

Mobile Task Forces are specialist units comprised of veteran field personnel drawn from all over the Foundation. These task forces are mobilized to deal with threats of a specific nature and can include anything from field researchers specializing in a particular type of anomaly to heavily armed combat units tasked to secure certain types of hostile anomalous entity. See the Task Forces document for more detailed information.

Administration

SITE DIRECTOR

Site directors for major Foundation facilities are the highest-ranking personnel at that location and are responsible for the continued, safe operation of the site and all of its contained anomalies and projects. All major departmental directors report directly to the Site Director, who in turn reports to the O5 Council.

O5 COUNCIL MEMBER

The O5 Council refers to the committee consisting of the highest-ranking directors of the Foundation. With complete access to all information regarding anomalies in containment, the O5 Council oversees all Foundation operations worldwide and directs its long-term strategic plans. Due to the sensitivity of their positions, O5 Council members must not come into direct contact with any anomalous object, entity, or phenomenon. Furthermore, the identities of all O5 Council members is classified; all council members are referred to only by their numeric designation (O5-1 through O5-13).

FACILITY DESIGNATIONS

The Foundation maintains and operates a large number of facilities worldwide, from small outposts with only a handful of staff to major Sites with thousands of personnel.

SITE
Foundation facilities designated as Sites are covert facilities, meaning that while existence of the facility is known to the public, such facilities are often disguised under government or corporate fronts. Sites are often built in locations in relatively close proximity to civilian populations, where facilities would require such cover.

AREA
Foundation facilities designated as Areas are clandestine facilities, meaning that civilians are not aware of their existence at all. Such facilities are often built far away from civilian populations and may contain highly dangerous anomalies; the vast majority of Areas have extreme fail-safe measures such as on-site nuclear warheads.
Facility Sections

SECTOR
Sectors are sections of Sites or Areas that are designated for specific purposes, such as containment, research, or storage. The exact usage of Sectors vary from facility to facility and is dependent on the facility's primary purpose and size.

UNIT
Units are self-contained sections of Sites or Areas such as those containing Biological or Dimensional anomalies and are designed to self-seal in case of a breach or other catastrophic event. All personnel entering or exiting a Unit must typically undergo a full decontamination procedure.

Prefixes
These prefixes are often used to denote specializations of facilities or facility sections and are generally only used in internal communication.

Armed

Armed denotes a facility or facility section with abnormally high physical security concerns, either due to containment of violent hostile entities or threat of outside attack. Such facilities typically have a large amount of military-grade weaponry and vehicles as well as a disproportionately large number of permanent security staff; in the case of a full facility, this typically entails a detachment of at least battalion or regiment strength.

Biological (Bio)
Biological containment facilities or facility sections deal with infectious or otherwise biohazardous anomalies and are both isolated and self-contained to prevent the possible escape of such anomalies.

Containment
Containment facilities or facility sections are primarily equipped and intended for the containment of anomalous objects, entities, or phenomena.

Dimensional (Dim)
Dimensional containment facilities or facility sections deal with extradimensional apertures or anomalies exhibiting inconsistent or warped spacetime.

Humanoid
Humanoid containment facilities or facility sections primarily deal with sentient, sapient human or near-human entities capable of understanding and complying with instructions. These are essentially analogous to a prison facility for anomalous entities.

Protected
Protected facilities and facility sections are "safe zones" kept free of anomalous influence. No anomalies are allowed within these facilities at any time.

Provisional
Provisional facilities are those that are established or built around an immobile anomaly. Provisional facilities typically contain only a single anomaly.

Reliquary
Reliquary facilities or facility sections are designed for handling artifacts and objects of religious or historical significance.

Research
Research facilities or facility sections are designed for either the handling and study of anomalies or anomalous materials or research and development of new containment schemes and methods.

Storage
Storage facilities or facility sections are intended for long-term storage of non-anomalous or inert anomalous objects with no risk of autonomous interaction.

Miscellaneous
These are Foundation facilities or locations that do not fall under the standard organizational structure.

Observation Posts
Observation Posts are tiny facilities established in a multitude of locations worldwide. Often limited to small standalone buildings or single units within larger buildings, Observation Posts are typically used to monitor regional communications for flagged content, as well as monitor nearby Foundation facilities. Many Observation Posts are also used as secure communications hubs or safe-houses by undercover Foundation agents.

YELLOWSTONE

The YELLOWSTONE facility acts as a training ground and housing for agents and personnel who are either not assigned or who are specialists. It also acts as a primary holding facility for recently acquired SCPs.

MOBILE TASK FORCES

Mobile Task Forces (MTFs) are elite units comprised of personnel drawn from across the Foundation and are mobilized to deal with specific threats or situations that sometimes exceed the operational capacity or expertise of regular field personnel and — as their name suggests — may be relocated between facilities or locations as they are needed. Mobile Task Force personnel represent the "best of the best" of the Foundation.

Mobile Task Forces vary greatly in size, composition, and purpose. A battalion-strength combat-oriented task force trained to deal with highly aggressive anomalous entities may consist of hundreds of troops plus support personnel, vehicles, and equipment and can be deployed in whole or in part to deal with threats across the globe. However, a Mobile Task Force can also be a small, specialized intelligence-gathering or investigative task force that may have fewer than a dozen personnel if that is deemed sufficient to accomplish their goals. While in the field, task force members often pose as emergency responders, local or federal law enforcement, or military personnel appropriate to the region in which they are operating. Mobile Task Force Commanders can also request the assistance of local field units or personnel stationed at nearby Foundation facilities in order to accomplish their missions.

ORGANIZATION

Each unit is fundamentally structured in a way that best suits their intended purpose. While combat-oriented task forces may closely follow military hierarchy and organization, smaller units may have an informal or otherwise esoteric chain of command. As such, the responsibilities of the Mobile Task Force Commander (MTFC) for each particular task force can vary greatly; the commander for a large task force might focus on maintaining multiple teams and deploying them as necessary to each assigned operation, whereas the commander of a small team might deploy with their team and direct the operation from on location.

Similarly, the cohesion of each unit will vary as well. Some Mobile Task Forces consist of personnel who have trained and worked for many years or even decades together, whereas the personnel of a Mobile Task Force formed on a moment's notice to deal with a specific incident may know little more than each others' names and fields of expertise.

CREATION
Mobile Task Forces are typically commissioned as deemed necessary by the Foundation's Director of Task Forces, often with the direct approval of one or more O5 Council members. A significant number of Mobile Task Forces are created to deal with specific anomalies exhibiting traits that standard containment or response teams are unable to effectively counteract, though many were also created to pre-empt an emerging or theoretical threat.

DEACTIVATION
Mobile Task Forces created for the purpose of containing a particular anomaly are typically deactivated at the end of the recovery operation or when ongoing containment is deemed no longer necessary. Occasionally, such task forces remain operational if the expertise and experiences learned are considered useful for future incidents, but otherwise the task force will likely be disbanded and its personnel returned to their prior posts. Very rarely, a Mobile Task Force will also be disbanded if it suffers sufficient casualties to render it incapable of operation. In these cases, if the prior capability of that

particular task force is deemed necessary, a new task force may be commissioned to replace it.

SPECIALIST AGENTS

Specialists are agents who operate as a one man MTF. As of [REDACTED] there is only one specialist active in the United States, this is J.Poole.

NAME : J. Poole
AGE : [REDACTED]
RACE: Caucasian
EYE COLOR: [REDACTED]
DISCERNING MARKS : [REDACTED]
RANK: Specialist
BASE OF OPERATIONS: Yellowstone
CLERANCE LEVEL : [REDACTED]

NOTES:

All personnel, excepting O-5, who are present during a hostile situation or field mission during which J.Poole is involved will obey any commands issued without question. Hesitation or refusal to obey commands will result in immediate termination.

Agent is to be equipped with
Standard field medical kit
Tranquilizers containing 1000cc of [Redacted]
Modified 1911
Modified Lincoln Town-car 19[Redacted] Model
Black suit coats
Black Ties

Black Shoes
Black gloves (Must be made of [Redacted]

PROLOGUE

"There is a house in New Orleans...", The radio drifted into static as Agent Johnathen Poole drove towards the lone post office in the town of Cora. Cora Montana to be exact, a small town right on the edge of Yellowstone national park and one of the least desirable places to live in the US. The midday sun was beating down on the weather worn blacktop when he finally pulled into the parking lot and climbed out of his sputtering Lincoln.

It was the kind of hot that can make sweat bead up on your neck and soak your shirt collar. Poole mused that it was probably almost as hot as Hell and let out a tired sigh. He walked around to the trunk of the old beat-up car and pulled out a large stainless steel ring of keys. Some looked brand new but others were just rusted hunks of metal. He whistled as he flipped through the keys, his fingers lingering on each one.

Anyone who drove by at that moment would have been forgiven for staring because it isn't often to see an actual G-Man. Now, what you need to understand is that when I write the word G-Man I am not talking about your fancy pant FBI agents or your suave CIA personnel. Nor am I referring to your IRS accountants, who are barely people in the first place. No, I mean a G-Man, tall and board shouldered with a pitch black suit and mirrored aviator sunglasses. They never smile or even grin in the presence of civilians and they ALWAYS wear black gloves. They also don't wear belts instead they favor clip on suspenders and a black clip-on tie complimented with a black fedora.

Poole was one of these eponymous G-Men, and he liked it. It wasn't so much that he didn't like people, more that people tended to dislike him. Not that he blamed them since he often even disliked himself. But there was one group he knew which liked him well enough, the foundation. He smirked as he passed over a key marked with their symbol, its circle with three arrows pointing inward was briefly reflected in his sunglasses. Finally, he stopped on the key for his Lincoln and inserted it into the trunks lock.

Poole took a deep breath and opened the trunk, the sickening waft of decomposing bodies hit him like a wall. With a grimace he reached in and grasped at the objects hilt and pulled out a rather normal looking umbrella. Poole held it away from his person as if it were radioactive and fished around with his free hand inside his shirt pocket. With a flourish and a shake, he pulled out an umbrella bag, the kind they use in big box stores, and stuffed the umbrella inside .

He slammed shut the lid of the trunk and muttered something about how they better be able to pay for repairs and a deep clean. With a grunt, he walked towards the squat stone building which housed the local post office and opened the front door. A cheery jingle played out over the PA system as he walked up to the service desk and sat the umbrella down on top of the counter. A plump maternal woman with granite gray hair smiled at him politely. Poole squinted behind his glasses and glanced down at her lap, he knew that under the counter she had a 12 gauge shotgun with tungsten carbide slugs pointed squarely at his testicles.

"Pleasant weather we are having isn't it?" She said as her arm almost imperceptibly adjusted her aim. "I only wish it was hotter," Poole said as he patted the umbrella. The woman seemed almost disappointed as she placed both hands on the counter and looked at the plastic covering the umbrella. "Poole, one day you're gonna forget to say the passcode and then I'm gonna to shoot you." She said with only a hint of humor in her voice. "I doubt you're that good of a shot," Poole muttered as he turned from the counter to lock the door.

At that moment an elderly woman walked in as he began to turn to lock the door. She lightly pushed him out of the way and hobbled her way up to the counter. "Young lady!" she squeaked in a shrill and uncomfortable tone, the bun of gray hair on her head bounced slightly as she spoke. Poole paused for a moment and grimaced and started to say something but by then agent at the counter was already talking to the elderly woman about how many stamps she wanted to buy. Poole was finally about to say something but before he could open his mouth the transaction was finished. That was when the old woman turned to leave...and knocked the umbrella to the floor.

It hit the ground with a heavy solemn thud, the plastic covering riding up over the handle. Poole and the agent at the counter met eyes briefly as the lady stared at the umbrella. "What kind of idiot would leave an umbrella on a mail counter," she whined as she knelt down to pick it up. Poole slowly began to reach into his suit coat, his fingers curling around the butt of a 1911 specially modified semiautomatic pistol. At the same time, the counter agent's arm slid under the counter to grasp at the shotgun.

The old woman's gnarled fingers wrapped around the umbrella and lifted it. It was then that she noticed how quiet it had gotten. "Is everything OK dea..." she didn't finish her sentence as her jaw began to extend downwards, popping and cracking as her facial bones shattered and snapped in a macabre symphony. The skin on her face was stretching grotesquely making her lips split as her teeth elongated, her eyes rolled back into her head until only the bone whites of her eyes showed as thick clot filled blood pooled around them and ran down her face leaving sanguine red tear streaks, her teeth ripped at their gums causing dark-red blood and stinking black bile to pour from her mouth.

The agent at the counter stared in mute horror as from the depths of her now gaping maw small arms began to reach out, children's hands worn gray from decay reached for her. The sounds of crying infants and screaming children began to seep from every facial orifice of the creature. The agent watched as the arms began to claw across the counter, spewing like elongated otherworldly tendrils from the monster's mouth. Behind them began to squeeze the unmistakable heads of children, the arms sprouting from their grotesquely distended mouths.

Like a crack of thunder Poole's pistol shot a single round through the hand holding the umbrella. The old woman fell to the ground screaming as the children's arms began to tear across the ground for the umbrella pulling her body like a rag-doll filled with viscera and fear. Poole, in a mad dash, grabbed the umbrella and flung himself over the counter. He dragged the horror stricken agent onto the ground next to him and grunted at her not to look. On the other side of the counter the hands, deprived of their property began to tear at the old woman's body. They peeled her skin off in bits and pieces, using their ragged and worn nails to scratch and cut. When her skin finally was flayed the hands began to rip chunks of her muscles and tendons free, like chimpanzees tearing the flesh of a melon from the rind.

Poole closed his eyes and let himself disconnect from the situation. He reminded himself she was someone he didn't know and that he must do what he can to protect the whole and not the one. Her screams grew louder, the cursed properties of the umbrella forcing her to stay conscious and alive, increasing her sensitivity to each new spark of pain. Her blood pooled around her on the floor and her own hands clawed at the linoleum. Her fingernails peeled from their nail-beds as she began to claw more frantically, unable to find purchase of the blood slicked floor. Finally, she went silent, and Poole stood up and let out a sigh.

Poole turned sharply from the scene and began to walk, umbrella in hand, towards the back of the room where a elevator stood waiting. Halfway there he heard muffled crying, looking back at the counter he saw the agent from the counter curled up against the wall with tears running down her blood-soaked face. "Get up and clean up this mess agent," Poole said in a calm and collected voice. She whimpered and shook her head, curling up tighter into a ball. "Clean it up or take that shotgun of yours and put in your resignation." He growled, his voice filled with a weary menace.

He then continued down the room and into the waiting elevator. As the doors closed he caught the briefest glimpse of the agents quivering hand reaching for the shotgun. As the elevator shuddered to life and began to descend smooth Jazz began to play and a recorded line started to play. "We at the SCP Foundation are always happy to welcome our guests/entities/employees and other beings. Please enjoy your stay at our facility and make sure to only be present in your designated areas! Once again, welcome to the SCP - Foundation facility 245 ;code named Yellowstone."

CASE 1 : SCP-056

Item #: SCP-056
Object Class: Euclid

Special Containment Procedures: SCP-056 is to be kept in a room of its choosing, with whatever furnishings it expresses desire for. Level 1 personnel and above may interact with SCP-056 at any time they choose, for a time length not exceeding two hours. The subject is to be guarded by a minimum of three (3) security staff at all times, with shift changes every four hours. Each guard is to be armed with non-lethal tranquilizer pistols, loaded with no less than fifteen hundred (1500) microliters of cyclopyrrolone tranquilizer. Any irregularities in personnel and staff developed by extended exposure to SCP-056 will result in psychological examination and relocation to site [DATA EXPUNGED].
The subject is to be allowed access to any object it desires, with the exceptions of weapons, communication devices, an internet connection, and other SCP objects. It may wander in Research Sector ▆ as it wills, but never allowed access to floors with exits. In the event of an emergency, or if SCP-056 becomes violent, it is to be subdued and contained within its room if possible. At no time should personnel attempt to harm SCP-056; see Addendum 2-b.

Description: SCP-056 is a being of variable size, gender, and appearance, which changes in response to the environment around it, especially in regards to living and sentient beings. Its most common form is of a handsome man in his middle twenties, dressed in a garb of similar appearance to that of the personnel guarding it but of a higher quality and aesthetic value. However, it has been recorded as taking these forms:
A large, well groomed Labrador Retriever (when exposed to Doctor ▆▆▆▆ ▆▆▆▆ 's dog).
A woman of similar appearance to famous actress Scarlett

Johansson when passing by a group of younger female staff. A female doctor in a white lab coat when speaking with various researchers. When asked to take an IQ test, the subject scored nearly thirty (30) points higher than the highest scoring researcher available.

A male bodybuilder, who was able to lift nearly two-hundred and fifty (250) kilogrammes twice on a bench press machine in the Sector's gym. This was thirty (30) kilogrammes heavier than the strongest security guard's maximum at the time.

A couch of extremely pleasing aesthetic value (when left alone in the subject's room).

These changes will generally occur the moment all people in the area lose focus on the subject, which occurs immediately upon exposure to a new object or person (See Addendum 3). Filming these changes has proved inconsequential, as any viewing the tapes or feed suffer the same momentary confusion. Clothing will also change during this time, though 056 has yet to manifest any sort of tools or weapons.

It is theoretically impossible to view SCP-056's original or "natural" form. When left in an empty, concrete cell and under closed-loop video surveillance, it took on the form of a higher quality camera, and appeared to monitor the camera watching it. Further attempts to yield its natural form discovered that when alone, it had no readable life signs, including body temperature, heart beat, or weight. It is assumed by researchers that it could not exist without any sort of perception.

Personnel in contact with the subject often report feeling "jealous" or "unsatisfied", yet will often give a great deal of both positive and negative attention to SCP-056, which can be predicted by their personality types. Security staff will often claim that they wish to follow the subject's commands, even if they dislike it or its current form, while researchers in extended contact with it will often try to argue and verbally abuse it, which usually results in the subject sending them out in shame. SCP-056 is quite capable of speech, and can apparently communicate in any language, verbal or not, and has shown fluency in over 200 dialects, including those invented by cryptographers and hobbyists. It frequently treats the staff around it with disdain, though is generally willing to do whatever is asked of it, so long as the inquiring does so in a submissive way. It expresses interest in magazines, fashion, automobiles, theoretical science, sports, and a multitude of other subjects, usually expressing greater knowledge and understanding of the topic than the person communicating with it. Personnel will generally become angry, disenchanted, or disgusted with SCP-056 after speaking with it for great lengths of time, though they will try to speak with it again if possible. When questioned about other SCPs, it showed fear and occasionally hatred, and refused to speak about any of them, even objects classified as Safe.

Additional: Subject was found to be working for the clothing design company [REDACTED], after an unusual number of homicides, suicides, and mental breakdowns of other models when working around SCP-056. When Class E personnel attempted to detain it, their mannerisms provoked it to change into what appeared to be the form of [DATA EXPUNGED] resulting in the deaths of seventeen (1) agent and ten (10) civilians. The incident was covered up by claiming an employee suffering from psychopathy brought a firearm to work and attacked other workers.

Addendum 1: refer to document #956-0.

Document #956-0: Audio recording of first encounter with SCP-056
<Begin Tape>
Agent ███████: Hey, listen up... whatever you are. You're under arrest for murder.
SCP-056: No. Go away.
(Clicking noises. Agent has drawn his weapon.)
Agent

J. Poole : Agent of the Foundation

██████████: You need to come with us right now.

SCP-056: You don't want to do that, you stupid little man.

(Expressions of surprise, presumably from onlookers)

Agent ██████████: The fuck? It looks just like [DATA EXPUNGED]!

(Gunshots and screaming)

<Tape ends>

Addendum 2-a: See document #956-1.

Document #956-1: Behavioral Testing for SCP-056

Testing Procedures:

[DATA EXPUNGED]

Addendum 2-b: Results:

One (1) male Class D Personnel, armed with knife. Intent: to harm subject. (Subject appeared as a lean, fit man of approximately twenty years of age. Subject proceeded to disarm and kill personnel.)

One (1) female Class D Personnel, bearing a bottle of fine wine. Intent: to offer subject gift. (Subject appeared as a beautiful woman, accepted the gift, and upon tasting, spit it back in the personnel's face before waving her away.)

Two (2) Class D Personnel, both male and female, carrying nothing and intending nothing. (Subject appeared as a beautiful woman in a well-tailored business suit. Examined both personnel, then dismissed them.)

Ten (10) Class D Personnel, all male, intending and carrying nothing. (Subject appeared as a beautiful woman, dressed in a low-cut red dress. After approximately ten minutes, all personnel began showing signs of irritation, and five minutes later broke out in fighting. Subject waved them away after watching them for seven minutes.)

One (1) female Level 4 Personnel, voted to be best looking woman on facility. Carried nothing, intended nothing. (Subject appeared as an extremely aesthetically pleasing woman, and displayed a large lexicon and understanding of management skills. Spoke to personnel for nearly ninety minutes, until personnel became infuriated and left the room.)

Addendum 3: Note from Doctor Kennith:
I was recently informed that 056 has repeatedly requested access to the internet. When I asked 056 about this, it told me that we were "unable to provide [it] with enough sycophants", and that it "wanted the whole world to know [its] face." Needless to say, its request was denied.

===

Poole woke up in a cold sweat, he was having nightmares again. He shook his head and stood up from his standard-issue army green fold-out cot, and glanced around for his slippers. After finding them he shuffled into the attached bathroom on his 'room'. The sound of electric clippers and running water was his morning theme song as he began his daily routine of shaving before sunrise. If you could call the lights being turned slightly brighter in an underground bunker 'sunrise' that is.

Poole, having shaved and showered shrugged into his office attire. A white dress shirt with black suspenders and a thin black tie, pinstripe pants with brown loafers completed the ensemble. His shoes slapped against the pavement as he left the 'room and started to walk through the corridors of the Yellowstone facility. He was headed towards the cafeteria when his cellphone began to ring. "Poole," he muttered into the phone as he got in line for breakfast with other agents jostling around him. "Agent Poole? This is McKowski, of the anomalous occurrences division. We just got alerted that an agent was killed in the field. We need someone to go in and locate the SCP responsible."

Poole grunted as he grabbed his tray, he shifted and balanced his cellphone on his shoulder and began to walk towards the nearest table. "Where is the subject located, and why aren't you sending in a team?" The line went quiet for a second and he could just make out McKowski relaying his question to her supervisor. "Knoxville Tennessee sir and management has decided that it would be better to utilize your... specialties for this mission as opposed to a full team." Poole mulled this over as he shoved a piece of bacon into his mouth. He swallowed, "fine".

He could hear Makowski's relieved grin on the other end of the phone, "Alright agent wheels up in two hours. We will be expecting you in the hanger and ready for your flight." Poole grunted in the affirmative and hung up, slamming his phone down onto the laminate surface of the table he leaned back and closed his eyes. He could feel a migraine starting behind his eyes and knew it would be a long day. With a screech of protest his chair slid back as he stood up and left, he had work to do.

A few hours later agent Poole walked out of the east terminal in Knoxville. From behind his mirrored sunglasses he watched as families met up with their loved one and businessmen waited for cars. He waited until all the other travelers had gotten their bags and left before he picked up his briefcase from the terminal's luggage claim. With a grunt, he picked up the leather-bound case and began to walk towards the concourse doors.

Waiting outside was his Lincoln, it sat under a nearby street lamp. The cone of light it made seemed to make the early morning shadows that much deeper. As Poole walked towards it the sun was just starting to rise over the small southern city. He opened up the trunk of his car and smirked when he saw that it was spotless, He tossed his briefcase in and slammed the trunk shut. It was then he felt like someone was watching him. Not just as if he was being stared at, no, this was the primal sense of dread and instinct. The hairs on the back of his neck began to stand up and his hand slowly moved towards his firearm. A cold sweat broke out on his forehead as he felt someone... something, creeping up behind him. A shuffling sound along the ground to his back left made him tense to turn around.

He glanced down as his hand closed around the butt of his pistol, and in the warped and blurred reflection of the Lincolns bumper, he saw something not entirely human behind him. Its form slid along the ground like some kind of creeping primordial creature towards him, its movements not of this earth and at the same moment wholly familiar in their horrifying simplicity. With practiced ease, Poole turned on his heel and aimed the gun at the creature, his sunglasses reflecting the sunrise. But there was nothing there.

Poole kept his eye on the spot where he had seen the... thing. He glared at it like a child trying to understand a 'magic eye' puzzle. Then he slowly began to back away, never letting his gaze waver. He fished his keys out of his pocket and climbed into the Lincoln, watching the spot in his rearview mirror. He turned the key in the ignition and began to drive. It wasn't until he was on the freeway that he let out a breath he didn't realize he had been holding.

Poole pulled into the Lazy Bear motel in south Knoxville around

J. Poole : Agent of the Foundation

7 in the morning, an hour after his flight had landed. The motel was a nice place, during the 1960s, but a series of murders and tax audits had turned it into a dump a raccoon would be ashamed to live in. When Poole walked into the room he made two mental notes. First, ask the people in the accounting department for a raise on his lodgings budget. Second, to get this job done as quickly as possible.

After checking the room for bugs, both the electronic kind and living kind, Poole brought in his briefcase. He tossed it onto the well-worn bed and opened it. He then pulled out a small black tablet and some other equipment, as he waited for it to power on he also opened the manila folder which held the file on his target. The creature had been designated SCP-056. From the recording that central had gotten from the last agents encounter it seemed to be able to shapeshift, but into what? He grimaced as he read over how they had found the agent's body in pieces, some of his organs had been liquefied into a slurry of bone, blood, and meat.

His tablet beeped at him and Poole turned it on eagerly. A database of all known folklore, mythology, urban legends, and secret conspiracies met his eyes. Poole began to shift through all the stories available to him, going over any mention of shapeshifters. He spent hours going through the old stories and legends, by the time he gave up the day had already turned to dusk. He stood up from the desk and stretched, his glasses showing him his pale reflection. Poole walked over to the rooms single window, with a sigh he leaned against the window frame. He watched out the dirty window as he chewed on a standard-issue rations bar. Something out there had killed a foundation agent, but what?

By the time true evening had fallen and its cloak of plutonian darkness and silence had fallen, Poole had been looking at the map of the last GPS coordinates of the previous agent for a few hours. A construction site in the theater district, close to the riverfront, was where they had found the body. The GPS locator had been found lodged into the concrete of a nearby wall, protected flesh that still surrounded it. Something about this didn't sit right with Poole, but he had no time to lose. Nighttime had come and he needed to be out there hunting this thing down.

Poole arrived at the riverfront construction site about an hour after the last worker had gone home. When he climbed out of his car the smell of stale cigarettes and sweat melded with the heady scent of wood and steel met him. After jumping a nearby fence he walked to the center of the construction site and began to survey his surroundings. The skeleton of the buildings and the stacks of materials and equipment cast deep and alien shadows across the moonlit landscape. In the distance, he could hear the scuttling of rats and the sound of rushing water. At the far end of the site, a large drain pipe (big enough for a car to drive through) gaped like the eye socket of a half-buried skull. The shadows deepened as the moon rose higher and his eyes shifted back and forth behind his mirrored glasses as he waited.

He was only there for a minute when he felt himself break out into a cold sweat. "So they sent someone else?" A chilling voice seemed to ring out from every shadow around him. A crushing feeling of dread made him pause and the blood in his veins turned to ice. Poole's hand started to go for his gun when he was sharply reprimanded by the same voice, "I wouldn't do that agent, your co-worker tried the same thing." Poole paused, his hand hovering above the butt of his pistol. "Then how do you suggest we solve this?" He could feel the creature watching him, just on the edge of his field of vision he caught a glimpse of movement. In the reflection of a nearby puddle of water, he could see something move across the night sky. It was only when he felt the chilled breath on his neck that he

J. Poole : Agent of the Foundation

began to be afraid.

"We see who is better, I am good at so many things so maybe you can provide me with a challenge. After all, there is something... special about you. What exactly are you?" Poole looked into the reflection of a nearby circular saw. In its muddy and scared surface, he could make out a form so alien and not of this earth behind him that it defied explanation. Poole grimaced and nodded "None of your damn business. If I play your game and win you come back with me to meet some friends of mine." The cold breath tittered in his ear and for a moment it sounded like a thousand voices whispering all at once, "You mean the Foundation? Oh yesssssss I am familiar with what they do, very very familiar."

The presence of the creature backed away and once again seemed to surround Poole. "Make it through the drainpipe to the other side, and you win" Poole raised an eyebrow at this. "Of course," the creature continued, "If you can't make it to the other side we will need to have a long conversation about how great I am. . . and then we can talk about how tasty you will be." Poole watched as from the shadows of the drain pipe a tall a beautiful woman walked out. She was wearing a red dress that shimmered in the moonlight, and her smile shined across the construction site. She turned on her heel and began to walk into the shadows, pausing only to glance over her shoulder as Poole began to follow.

Poole walked into the
 drainpipe with little trouble and soon was up to his ankles in brown and black water. All around him the darkness and the stone walls closed in, like a stone coffin. He knew from his research that the tunnel continued for about the length of two football fields before coming out onto the University of Tennessee's campus. Poole pulled his suit coat tight around him and pushed deeper into the tunnel. As the moonlight

disappeared into the blackness behind him he felt the presence return. "What are you? I know you aren't all human, that much is obvious, but what are you?" Poole smiled as the creature kept asking again and again as he went deeper. A few moments later it's presence seemed to dissipate into the shadows and he was alone.

In the distance a young woman leaned against the wall, sobbing as she clutched the blood-stained hem of her dress. Poole walked past her without stopping, only grunting out a compliment saying it was a nice try but not his type. With a screech of pain and shock, the girl rounded on him, "What the fuck are you!?" Its arms split into four appendages each limb ending in three rapidly extending fingers. The legs seemed to buckle and curve up over it's back as its arms spread out. The tendons of each appendage stretching with a sickening twang and dripping bloody flesh. Poole silently watched her as she dropped onto her four arms and began to scuttle across the ground towards him as if some kind of mutated cyclopean beetle. Her eyes popped out of their sockets and seem to rise as if on stalks made of their optic nerves, each strand glistening in the almost pitch blackness of the tunnel. The creatures rushed at him with blinding speed, and Poole turned and began to run.

The water made it difficult for him to get speed, it seemed to suck at his feet and slow him down at every turn. However, through sheer determination, he was able to outrun the creature and her screams faded into the dark. Poole paused for a moment to collect his thoughts as he leaned against the wall in the dark tunnel. As he did this he began to feel something dark in the shadows, his breath came out in a fog and he suddenly had the urge to run again. "Am I not beautiful?" The voice said all around him. Poole shook his head and began to push forward, he had lost count of his steps and now he couldn't remember how many yards he had left to go.

J. Poole : Agent of the Foundation

He walked for what seemed like hours through the wet and the dark. Each step draining his strength. Until he saw a light up ahead, it was a hole in the wall. He approached it slowly and slid along the wall until he was directly beside the opening. Poole took off his glasses and using the reflective surface peered into the room beyond. It was a dry and dusty waiting room, it looked like it hadn't been touched since the early 20th century. On the bright side, it was empty and dry so Poole turned and walked in. He looked around as he walked into the waiting room and noticed a calendar on the wall which as dated for October 1916.

The room was lit by the light of several oil lanterns and the door on the other side of the room was ajar. He looked around slowly as his eyes acclimated to the bright light source. After a few moments, he approached the door to the second room and slowly pushed it open with his shoulder. It was a small office with a desk and a nameplate that said, "Mrs. Burnell Kushing: Women's Fashion Designer." In the corner was a mirror made of well-worn brass, it was the only thing in the room that wasn't covered in a thick layer of dust.

Poole closed the door with a grunt and walked to the mirror, by the flickering light of the rooms single oil lamp he looked weather-worn and old. Like a veteran of a war that has gone on for too long. He smirked as he looked at himself and adjusted his fedora. "you like how you look?" The voice said, its crushing presence knocking the wind out of Poole. He stumbled forward and leaned against the mirror, attempting to get away as the cold and the pressure began to increase. "Look at yourself now," the creature said with an audible sneer, "You are fucking pathetic." Poole pushed himself up and looked at his reflection. His skin had gone pale and his sunglasses had fallen off when he stumbled.

His breath was coming out in short bursts, turning to fog the second it came in contact with the cold air. He glanced around the room frantically searching for the source of the voice and his glasses. The creature began to laugh, its cackle bordering on a hyena-like laugh. But he couldn't see anything and as the pressure increased the oil lamps began to dim. Poole turned and leaned against the cool surface of the mirror and screwed up his eyes. It was only when the pressure stopped growing that he opened his eyes to look at his reflection, and it flashed a grin filled with sharpened needle-like teeth at him.

His reflection lunged from inside the mirror at Poole's neck. He felt the thousands of little teeth sink into his jugular and he fell to the ground with a gurgle as the creature twisted and tore. The mirror and the creature twisted and swirled until it was the woman in the red dress kneeling over him, blood pouring from her chin and down her neck and breasts. Her jaw grotesquely stretching and her eyes pitch black. The monster leaned down and sniffed along the edge of the bite and began to whisper in his ear. Poole kept his eyes closed and could feel his body start to go numb. Then he took a deep breath and looked at the creature as its mouth opened impossibly wide, and thousands of barbed tongues began to extend towards his cut.

It was right here that Poole started to chuckle and a smile broke out across his face. The creature stopped and stared at the laughing agent. It reared back a fist and punched him directly in the face, "SHUT UP!" Poole was laughing so hard now that blood spurted from his neck and tears poured down his cheeks. The creature glared at Poole and then began to sway, "What the fuck... what did you do to me!" It screamed as Poole rolled away and peeled off the flesh-colored neck guard.

Poole stood up and shook himself, placing two fingers on either side of his nose he cracked it back into place. "Did you know that most predators go after the neck?" He said as he re-lit the oil lamp, the pressure and cold was dissipating. He touched his face for a moment and grunted as he pulled off the contacts covering his eyes, one of them had ripped. The creature swayed as it fell to its knees and looked at him in abject horror. "It was a calculated risk I will admit but enough rhino tranquilizer and Rohypnol and anything should go down. Even a fucking monster like you." His eyes looked unflinchingly into the gaze of the monster, and it screamed as it held his gaze. It screamed and screamed until it ran out of air, tears ran down the creatures face and pooled around it as Poole's grin grew bigger.

The creature shrank back from Poole as he knelt, "You know what the best part is? I figured out your weakness before you even knew I was here." The creature began to shift from a woman to a child and started to cry. "Don't kill me, I was just so hungry" The little boy begged as Poole stood up and put on his sunglasses. "Oh I'm not going to kill you, your life is about to get so so much worse." The creature lunged at Poole with a scream, its mouth distending as its jaw widened and filled once more with needle-like teeth.

Like a solid block of stone Poole brought his foot down on the head of the creature. He pressed harder as it begged and cried to be let go. He pressed harder when it cried for its mother, and when it finally fell silent... he pressed harder.

Two days later there would be news that an underground gas pocket had caused an explosion in Knoxville. Twenty-two construction workers died and fifteen civilians were injured. Meanwhile, a new resident was added to the Yellowstone facility, and the next morning Poole sat down and finished his breakfast.

CASE 2 : SCP-097

Item #: SCP-097
Object Class: Euclid

Special Containment Procedures: SCP-097 is contained within the limits of the property where it was initially discovered, Zone-SCP-097. The property is surrounded by an 8 metre tall concrete block fence, fitted with barbed wire and security camera systems. Satellite images of Zone-SCP-097 are to be doctored, removing all traces of the area.

Any and all new plant growth outside the containment area suspected to originate from within the SCP is to be sterilized through application of boiling saltwater and/or incinerated. Absolutely all abnormal behaviour is to be reported to Doctor Bridge within ten minutes of occurrence. If any personnel or their families experience hallucinations or thematically related dreams outside of containment, they are to contact Doctor Bridge to schedule treatment.

Localities surrounding SCP-097, specifically [REDACTED], are to be monitored from the first of April until the first of November every year for affected civilians. Medical establishments dealing with sleep abnormalities are to be monitored for signs of SCP-097's influence. Civilians below the age of 16 encountered alone within 1 square kilometre of Zone-SCP-097 are to be taken into Foundation custody and are to be treated with a Class B amnestic and returned home, or the nearest police station. Personnel tasked with the return of civilians are to avoid public exposure; each Agent is to be assigned a cover story to follow if they do encounter civilians en-route to their destinations. See Level 3 staff for details.

The morning after the first frost of the year, a team of twenty-five Agents armed with agricultural tools are to enter SCP-097 and clear away the outer plant matter. This process is not to continue past dusk.

J. Poole : Agent of the Foundation

Description: SCP-097 is a ten acre area of land in the state of [REDACTED], in the Midwestern United States. It is the abandoned remains of the [REDACTED] County Fair 1969, an area of approximately 2.3 km2 (approx. 5.4 sq. mi). Structures within the SCP area exist in a state of moderate disrepair, consistent with the expected age and environment.

At the centre of SCP-097 lie the remains of a 1956 GMC pickup truck, majority of which is crushed beneath a colossal pumpkin of unknown subtype, henceforth SCP-097-01. SCP-097-01 stands approximately 7.4 metres (24.3 feet) tall and 8.1 metres (26.8 feet) in diameter at its widest. Current estimates put SCP-097-01 at approximately 15,000 kilograms (approx. 33,070 pounds). This pumpkin remains roughly spherical in shape, instead of spreading out under its own weight as would be expected of a plant of its size.

The remaining portion of SCP-097 (approx. 2 km2) is overgrown with several dozen varieties of pumpkins, with over seventy subspecies yet identified, and many previously unknown to agriculture. Many of these pumpkins have been shown capable of growing to enormous sizes, the average estimated weight being around 250 kilograms (avg. 550 lbs). These pumpkins, along with the assorted other crops, grow with, on and around the remains of the 1969 fairgrounds, creating a mazelike arrangement of plant life. The average height of the "walls" within SCP-097 is 1.6 metres, though this may vary from year to year.

Between April and November each year, the area within SCP-097 has produced a number of anomalous phenomena ranging from benign to implicitly aggressive. To date, seventeen Agents have been severely maimed within SCP-097, eight having died. See Event Log SCP-097 for a brief listing of recorded phenomena.

Addendum - Historical Note: Prior to the construction of SCP-097's containment wall, instances of what are now known as SCP-2171-1 were occasionally observed to form fragmented 'walls', and at one point a near-complete ring, of 2171 around SCP-097's area of effect. This behavior ceased following the containment wall's completion. The purpose and implications behind this interaction are as of yet unknown.

Effects of SCP-097 on Children: In addition to its immediate effects outlined in Event Log SCP-097, SCP-097-01 appears to produce an undetectable signal towards children in an undetermined range. For clarity, "children" will refer to individuals up to the age of 8 10.

Beginning in early April, civilian children within SCP-097's undefined range may be overcome with somnambulism on clear nights. Affected children will move around their homes, stopping to face closed doorways for several seconds before moving to the next nearest doorway, eventually returning to bed. At first, this behaviour will occur only once a week, beginning with only the doors on a single floor. This sleepwalking will become more frequent, by mid-August happening every night. If forcibly awoken at any time during these episodes, they will scream for several seconds before succumbing to a degree of confusion. After an affected child is awoken in this manner, the effect will cease, and the child will never show any further signs of SCP-097's influence.

Over the course of two to three months, these episodes will become more thorough, affected individuals seeking out each doorway inside their home, as well as those on their household's property, such as garages, car doors, and fence gates; eventually, they will begin visiting the front doors of neighbours. Beginning in September, affected children who have remained undisturbed during these episodes will begin to remain outside at sunrise, laying on grass near their homestead and returning to full REM sleep. Affected children may recall dreams centering around autumn activities.

Between September 1st and November 1st, if the affected children have not been awoken during the preceding sleepwalking episodes, they will cease the previously established activity during the sleepwalk, and instead begin to walk directly towards SCP-097's location. They will travel over fields and down secondary roads, steadily moving towards SCP-097. Local geography consists mostly of undeveloped Foundation-owned property, facilitating uninterrupted travel. Upon arrival at SCP-097, an affected child will sit down before SCP-097-01 and begin singing unidentifiable gibberish as music begins to play. While a number of instruments have been recorded, simple drums and pipes are the most consistently encountered.

After several minutes, childlike entities will crawl out from tangled flora, or break out of larger pumpkins within SCP-097. The children will be wearing whatever they were last seen with, most often pyjamas or similar clothing. Many of these entities match those children known to be lost to SCP-097-01.

The entities will surround the affected civilian child, dancing and singing in a circle as SCP-097-01 begins to emit dim light. The affected child will awaken, normally expressing a great deal of terror; the instant any vocalization is produced, the entities will swarm and kill the child. Methods used are different in each instance, but usually involve dismemberment or strangulation. At this point, any and all efforts to interrupt the entities will fail, whether through breakdown of equipment, sudden intangibility of the subjects, or express violence on the part of SCP-097.

After the death of the affected child, SCP-097-01 will split open and the entities will hurl the remains into it, before climbing in themselves. SCP-097-01 will then close, and the music will stop.

Before the containment wall was erected, at least ██ children between the ages of 3 and 10 are known to have been lost to SCP-097.

This is a general incident log for SCP-097 for the cycle between 09/01/ and 11/01/.
This is an abridged version; please requisition full individual reports from Dr. Bridge. During this time, four civilian children were captured and returned to their families.

Month/Day/Year
Time

Event

Notes

09/03/
09:39

Cameras 3b, 4a, 4c, 5b view child, approx. 4 years of age, walk between tangles of plant matter toward SCP-097-1 over an 8 minute period. Child appeared to be dragging a stuffed animal. Child appeared on footage during review period. No figure was viewed at the time of recording.

09/05/
17:33

Human scream heard from within SCP-097, heard throughout the site. On-site personnel described it as possessing a small child's voice. Sustained for approx. 3 minutes before stopping abruptly.
Staff reported feeling as if they were being watched during the event.

09/08/
-

Several "bed sheet ghosts" are seen through various security feeds throughout the day. Would only appear for approx. 1-3

J. Poole : Agent of the Foundation
seconds before vanishing again. Staff did not report seeing any
anomalous entities first-hand.
Patrols doubled for the remaining time in the SCP's cycle.

09/13/
22:19
Unidentifiable singing is heard throughout the Site, persisting
for three hours before becoming silent. Recordings reveal
songlike gibberish, with up to 30 individual children's voices
singing at any time.
Recordings archived for future study.

09/19/
14:27
Agent McRoy cuts a pumpkin's vine with machete; severed
vine proceeded to bleed approx. 50 litres of human blood
before shriveling.
Blood type AB-, no DNA match.

09/24/
-
Overnight, two separate pumpkin patches grew into the rough
approximations of humanoid figures, lying on the ground.
Destroyed without incident.

09/25/
05:17
Agent Long found decapitated, neck against a pumpkin.
Disappeared en-route to a restroom break.

09/27/
02:50
All light bulbs on-site burn out within a 2 minute period.
Critical areas repaired before nightfall.

09/30/

Steven L. Stamm

12:16
Sudden shift noted in the location of several dozen gourd plants.
Time and nature of actual event unknown.

10/01/████
14:29
Agent Cole accidentally damages and breaks pumpkin during weekly examination of SCP-097. Pumpkin splits open, revealing a complete human child's skeleton in the fetal position within.
Female, approx. 5 years old. No DNA match.

10/02/████
-
Twenty-nine (29) freshly decapitated crows (Corvus brachyrhynchos) found outside SCP-097's containment wall.
None.

10/06/████
06:37
Matured pumpkin plant found to have replaced a potted plant growing inside Dr. Bridge's office.
Indoor plants banned from the Site. Pumpkin incinerated immediately.

10/07/████

16:50

Agent Matthews falls unconscious during patrol and cannot be awoken until removed from property.

Agent reported dreaming of autumn colors and the smell of

J. Poole : Agent of the Foundation
leaves. Full recovery. Reassigned to desk work pending examination.

10/11/███
07:38
Research Assistant Sturm reports overwhelming taste and scent of pumpkin permeating her senses. No other personnel report anomaly.
Transferred off-site, examination pending.

10/13/███
-
Sounds of steady drums playing throughout the day, from 00:00 to 23:59.
Source of sound unknown. Recordings archived for future study.

10/17/███
03:19
Male child, approx. 6 years of age and clad in pyjamas, seen climbing through cornstalks on the eastern end of SCP-097, moving towards SCP-097-01.
Lost to SCP-097-01. How the child was able to escape notice by personnel until after he was lost to the SCP is unknown.

10/20/███
13:07
All personnel within 3.6 kilometres of SCP-097-01 report hallucinations of orange haze and children's laughter.
Personnel evacuated to a distance outside the area of effect.
Personnel screened for mental interference.

10/23/███
00:01
All power and backup power to the area failed. Upon recovery,

█ pumpkins within SCP-097 were found to have changed into carved lanterns.
It is unknown how SCP-097 generated and lit candles. Team-097-alpha and -beta tasked to destroy lanterns after sunrise.

10/23/
08:13
Team-097-alpha reports seeing and hearing children playing among the flora within SCP-097. Recordings lack the entities expected from the reports.
Children noted to be clad in pyjamas. Teams pulled from SCP. Screened for mental interference.

10/25/
11:49
Zea mays indurata kernels fall from the sky around SCP-097. Does not fall within containment walls.
Area cleansed with flame units and replanted with non-native grasses. Pavement of outside area pending.

10/26/█
21:13
Research Assistant O'Toole overcome with nausea and vomits pumpkin seeds. O'Toole did not eat pumpkin seeds previous to vomiting.
Research Assistant O'Toole transferred to Site █ for examination. Seeds incinerated with prejudice.

10/27/
10:03
Research Assistant O'Toole reported to have died overnight. Autopsy reveals thoracic cavity was filled with pumpkin seeds. Body incinerated at Site █. All personnel scheduled for full physical examination.

J. Poole : Agent of the Foundation
10/28/█████

-

Unintelligible whispering gibberish heard by fertile female personnel throughout the area when in view of SCP-097. Phenomenon continues throughout the day, continuing for the duration of SCP-097's cycle, i.e. until Nov 1.
Associated personnel removed from duty and scheduled for examination.

10/28/█████
17:45
Headlights of vehicle underneath SCP-097-01 light and stay lit until daybreak.
None.

10/29/█████

-

Fruit trees within SCP-097 blossom over the course of 5 hours beginning at roughly 07:00. Flowers wither and fall soon after.
None.

10/29/█████
08:07
Pumpkins near south entrance to SCP-097 began spontaneously bleeding from the stem. Each continued bleeding for three hours.
Blood type AB-, no DNA match.

10/31/█████
03:10
Several dozen unidentified spheres of red light viewed drifting above SCP-097 and surrounding area. When light was shone directly on the spheres a piercing shriek was heard.
Personnel called into the main building until the spheres dissipated at dawn.

Steven L. Stamm

10/31/█████

12:00

Sounds of steady drums are recorded from within SCP-097.
Drums persist for the following 12 hours.
No source identified. Recordings archived for future study.

10/31/█████

14:19

All strawberry plants within SCP-097 wither in unison.
None.

10/31/█████

17:43

Between twenty-five and thirty animate human skeletons of
varying size are recorded breaking out of larger pumpkins
within SCP-097. Skeletons traverse through SCP-097's flora to
the north-east peach tree and hang themselves from its
branches using lengths of grape vine, electrical cable, and
decaying rope. Skeletons ceased anomalous behavior after
pantomiming death by hanging; death throes continued for
approximately 23 minutes.
Skeletons recovered after first frost; all appeared under 12
years of age, no DNA matches. Skeletons incinerated after
examination.

==

Dr. Adriana Hart wasn't your average SCP doctor. Due to the
special needs of her child and her brilliance she had been
authorized to continue raising him under a special allowance by
the 0-5 council. It was an unfortunate oversight which resulted
in her being assigned to work with SCP-097. This amused
some people who found the idea of someone missing that

J. Poole : Agent of the Foundation

humorous. Poole didn't find it humorous and he especially didn't find it humorous when he was interrupted while cleaning his 1911.

His hands glided over the well worn stainless steel slide of his semiautomatic. The oil on the cleaning rag glistened under the fluorescent lights and its heavy scent lingered in the air briefly after every pass. Poole silently worked his weapon over as the other agents in the machine shop watched him wordlessly. It was rare he would even be out among them except to eat, but the last SCP had made him reconsider the benefits of an easy to draw and chamber pistol.

He had just replaced the firing pin when he heard a cough from over his left shoulder. "Yes?" he said in a voice barely above a murmur. "Poole," it was one of the representatives of the O-5 council. A tall lanky man so skeletal and thin that he looked almost dead. His hands and fingers extended and seemed more like talons than actual appendages. Light glistened sickeningly from his pale skin as he spoke, "The council has a special job for you Poole."

Poole wasn't impressed and continued to work on his pistol, "then tell the council they can call me." The tall man grimaced, his face curling up into a sneer as if he had just eaten a particularly sour piece of candy. "You would do well to remember who your employers are agent." Poole sat up straight on the stool he was using as a seat, "Your right..." He stood and turned to face the thin man, he towered over him and Poole could smell the fear leaving the man's pores. "As should you", Poole held his hand out to the man, who shakily placed a manila dossier in his outstretched palm.

"T-t-that's all agent, the council expects results immediately." Poole looked at him over the rim of his sunglasses, "I am aware of that, thank you." The thin man swallowed hard and noticed that while they had been speaking the other agents had left the room. Poole turned back to his table and began to re-assemble his gun, his fingers moving with practiced ease. The thin man backed away slowly and then turned and ran for the door. Sprinting through it and slamming it shut as he left.

Poole sat the dossier on the table as he slid the final pieces of his pistol back together. With a smooth metallic click, he drew back the modified slide and grinned as it snapped back into place. He aimed the pistol at his shadow and muttered,'bang'. Then he leaned back on the stool and sighed as he sat his weapon down and flipped open the dossier. Inside was a picture of Dr. Hart posing with a young boy who couldn't have been older than ten years old. Poole's eyes lingered on the picture for longer than he would have liked before he pushed it out of the way and began to read through the file on the SCP.

It was a long file, longer than most of the others. He read through the event logs and looked at the autopsy pictures, only stopping when his aching eyes and an intercom page told him it was time to go. He stood up and tossed the dossier into a nearby garbage can and pulled out his lighter. It was an old weather-beaten flip lighter from the second world war. It was scared and rusted but still worked even though the lids hinge liked to squeak when it was flipped open. Poole set the dossier on fire and watched it burn.

Poole walked out into the Yellowstone hanger and looked at the helicopter in front of him. He couldn't help but smile slightly, he felt like a stereotype. He was an agent of an organization that didn't exist riding in a black helicopter, he couldn't be happier. He climbed into the helicopter and strapped himself in while gazing out the window into the night. A misting rain had started outside and he watched as the droplets clung to the window, sliding down and into oblivion.

J. Poole : Agent of the Foundation

In all honesty, Poole hated the smell of the rain, it was too damp and heavy. By the time the helicopter landed near the site of SCP-097 what had started as a sprinkle became a downpour. With a grunt, he stepped down from the side of the helicopter onto the asphalt landing pad and looked around. All around him white tents and double-wide trailers were arranged around a chain-link fence topped with barbed wire. Above every doorway and on every tent flap words describing the activities within were stenciled in stark white letters. Poole looked around until he saw what he was looking for, the trailer that had MEDIC emblazoned on its door frame in big white letters.

As he walked towards the door he felt eyes on him from beyond the chain-link fence. This wasn't like the last mission he was on, these felt more like curious eyes than something that wanted to eat him. He shivered and quickened his pace towards the trailer as the rain began to pour in sheets all around him. By the time he reached the door, the ground around the camp had turned to an almost soup-like mush and water was dripping off of the brim of his hat.

Without knocking Poole entered into the medic bay.

The room was a sterile whitewash, with bright lights shining so brightly as to hurt a normal person's eyes. Along one wall a row of hospital beds sat and small machines beeped rhythmically. Poole walked past these towards the only other person in the room. At a small desk in the back corner sat a man who couldn't have been more than twenty years old. He had sandy blond hair and dark circles under both eyes. His face was gaunt but in such a manner as to suggest sleep deprivation and not malnutrition. "Doctor Darling?" Poole said in a tone that suggested it was less a question and more a method to wake the man up. "Ah agent," Darling tried to stand up but Poole motioned for him to sit. "My apologies agent I would stand but it seems that I may have overextended myself for the moment." Poole looked at him and nodded solemnly, "I would have to agree." Darling seemed relieved to hear this and leaned back.

"So you're here about Hart?" Poole nodded and Darling continued " She is a damn fool and should have left her kid at home. But she insisted he be brought along, the O-5 should have never allowed her..." "Careful doctor, " Poole said, his tone gentle but laced with deep malice. "Of course," Doctor darling shifted uncomfortably, "What I mean to say is she shouldn't have abused her special allowance. And that brings us to the here and now." Poole looked down at a clock on Darling's desk, "When did she enter the SCP after him?" Darling looked at his clock, "About two hours before sunset." Darling reached over and began to flip through a binder on his desk.

"Her son made it through the fence about three hours beforehand." Poole nodded silently and shifted his weight, "I better wait until morning then." Darling nodded and was about to say something when a soldier walked in. "Doc I need your..." the soldier fell to the ground screaming and clutching at his ears. Poole drew his handgun staring as Dr. Darling looked on apathetically. "Its hopeless agent, by the time they make it here it's too late." Darling looked at the soldier on the floor who was still screaming, "I'm sorry Simon, truly I am"

Simon screamed as blood began to seep between his fingers, his eyes bugged out from his skull as if trying to escape some unimaginable pain. He began to thrash and twist like a marionette on a string and after a moment his body went rigid, flexing itself off of the floor. "Fuck" Poole said as he watched. Simon's hands fell from his ears and green vines began to seep out of them. They were curled leafy things and would have seemed in place within a garden, save for the dark red blood which dripped from their leaves and the way the tendrils

J. Poole : Agent of the Foundation
swayed as they caressed his body.

Then one tendril drew back from the others and plunged
forward, puncturing into his body like a hypodermic needle.
Poole could see it under his skin, like a raised line that kept
growing longer, sliding between the layers of skin and fat,
spreading out in different directions. Poole watched as Simon
turned and looked at Poole his eyes flashing towards the gun
and mouthing the word, "Please." Poole leveled his arm and
fired one shot through Simon's head, his brains splattered out
behind him in a fine pink mist. Simon's body went limp like a
doll and Darling sighed as the vines wilted away.

Poole slept fitfully that night and in the distance, he could just
make out the sound of singing. The next morning he walked
into the Spec-ops tent and sat down with one Commander
Murphy. He was a man who was maybe a few years out from
retirement, his gray hair was buzzed short and his eyes were
steel gray. "You will of course want us to come along right?"
Murphy said as he sipped on his morning coffee, Poole had
walked in before breakfast and he was doing his best to
maintain some semblance of normal around the imposing
agent. "No," Poole said as he leaned back with his sunglasses
reflecting the room. "No?" Murphy was confused and sat his
mug down, "You are aware of what is beyond the fence right?"
Poole turned his head and seemed to glare in the direction of
the SCP, "I am especially aware of this commander, which is
exactly why I will be going in alone. But I will require one thing."
Poole took a small piece of paper and passed it to the
Commander.

Murphy looked at the paper and then at Poole, "you're
serious?" Poole nodded in the affirmative and stood up from
the camping stool he had been sitting on. "Agent you know this
is, well it will require 0-5 authorization to use" Poole paused for
a moment and then shrugged, "I am aware, talk to your site

supervisor...I expect it within the hour." Poole walked out of the tent and let the flap fall shut with a water-heavy thud. The misting rain had abated while he was in there and Poole took a deep breath and smirked, he had work to do.

The klaxon siren sounded as personnel surrounded the single gate in the fence, the gate slowly slid open revealing a hole in the armor which separated the camp from what was within. Poole stepped forward and hefted a backpack onto his shoulder. "If I'm not back by sunrise you need to contact the 05 councils, they need to nuke this place." Murphy grimaced at this and nodded as Poole began to walk through the gate. After the first few paces into the forest, the sounds of the camp disappeared to be replaced by the sound of an immense silence save for the songbirds.

Poole walked for what seemed like hours, he recalled something about how the effects of the area could be problematic for his mission. Eventually, he decided to stop and take a moment to refresh himself and to relive his bladder. As Poole stood with one hand against a tree and the other... 'aiming' he noticed something. The sounds that he thought were birds chirping was something else entirely. He finished and zipped himself up and then closed his eyes and listened.

As if conducted by some sadistic composer the sounds seemed to be a whispering chorus of young children's voices. Their songs were complete gibberish, like that of a fevered madman who has seen too much. Poole focused on the sounds and was dismayed to realize he couldn't pinpoint the location of the haunting melody of unintelligible madness.

He grunted in irritation and hefted his backpack onto his shoulders and continued, each footstep seeming to fall into rhythm with the low chanting. Eventually, Poole reached the edge of the fairgrounds, he paused for a moment and looked over the scene. In the center of the grounds there sat a giant orange pumpkin. It looked like something out of a child's cartoon it was so huge. Underneath it, a pickup truck was crushed with just the front end of the cab jutting out at a comically appropriate angle. All around this giant gourd smaller pumpkins (about the size of beach balls) seemed placed at random.

Poole counted and stopped after reaching one hundred, this wouldn't be something he could simply shoot his way out of or fight with a gun. He almost subconsciously touched the strap of his backpack and grinned a grim smile. Silently his eyes scanned the field for a sign of the doctor, but he couldn't find any. Poole frowned at this and sat down and leaned against a nearby oak tree. He sat the backpack between his legs and wrapped one loop around his arm, then he waited.

Nighttime came quicker than he would have liked. The sun which had been shinning bright when he sat down was now dipping below the horizon, casting a blood-red autumn hue across the surrounding area. The chanting had gotten progressively louder and Poole was getting annoyed. He lifted himself off the ground and slid the backpack back onto his person. Poole silently watched as the sun steadily sunk further over the horizon and an unearthly light began to emanate from the pumpkin patch.

The eerie green light made the shadows around Poole grow deeper and darker. He stepped back and sank into the inky blackness and watched from its hidden depths as a macabre scene began to unfold before him. The light seemed to make the shadows dance as the large pumpkin in the center began to split open until it seemed as if a child had crudely carved a large smile into its flesh. Stinking rotten pumpkin innards dripped from the jagged edges in an orange viscous manner and seemed to pool around it on the ground. Red glowing orbs of mist and light descended from the sky and settled into a position where the eyes would have been.

With the sound of wet rending plant matter, like someone smashing an overripe pumpkin, the surrounding pumpkins seemed to split as if one by one. The creatures that crawled forth from their depths seemed to almost unfold into the size of a small child. They were gray and gangly, emaciated beyond logical ability to operate. From a distance, they could have been mistaken for skeletons covered in a grayish-green paper-thin skin. From their ears and eyes, thick long leafy tendrils spewed and grew. These vines like growths wrapped around their necks, and as they moved Poole could make out that they held their bodies together. The growths acting almost as external tendons and muscles holding together the quartered remains of these lost souls.

Their fingers were tipped by long black nails, the beds upon which they rested had decayed long ago giving them an almost talon-like appearance. They were all, each and everyone, coated in a residue of blood and other bodily fluids. Poole watched silently as these creatures began to circle the giant pumpkin and sing enthusiastically. They raised their hands to the now rising moon and swayed as they sang in children's voices, each chanting a hauntingly sweet but dark melody of insanity and disjointed words.

On the edge of the pumpkin patch, about 200 yards from Poole, a young boy stumbled out of the darkness. His eyes were glazed over as he walked towards the pumpkin and the crowd. He was the same boy from the dossier, but he looked like he had just spent the better part of a day walking through a forest. His plaid pajamas were cut in multiple places and his feet were bloodied and missing toenails. He walked gingerly as if he had twisted his ankle. He stumbled forward with lifeless eyes, as if asleep.

J. Poole : Agent of the Foundation

As he neared the group they stopped singing and spread out as if to welcome him. The red mist like eyes of the large pumpkin seemed to follow him as he moved across the field. "NO!", Poole's eyes darted across the field to see Dr. Adriana Hart sprinting across the field as she screamed. Her face was a pale mask of panic and terror and she made it halfway to her son before the vines that carpeted the ground roared to life and encircled her, pinning her to the ground. Her fire-red hair spreading out in a halo around her head s she struggled to break free.

Poole watched as she screamed for her son to wake up, tears of impotent rage streamed down her face as every curse she could think of flew from her lips. Poole stepped out of the shadows after a moment and began to stride across the field. The vines around him seemed to writhe and squirm like snakes. One-shot out and wrapped itself around his leg and Poole stopped for a moment, then he reached down with one gloved hand and ripped the vine off his leg. Blood from the broken leaves and stem spurted out and began to spray around him making the other vines writhe in excitement.

Poole calmly walked up to the doctor and stared down at her. He glanced back at the boy who was nearing the group of creatures. "Fucking do something!" Dr. Hart screamed at the agent as she watched her son walk to his death. Poole silently looked at her and then back at the boy. "I'm not here for him." She froze at that and looked at Poole, her large blue eyes filling with both fear and tears. "By order of the foundation your contract is terminated," Poole said as he drew his 1911 and drew back the slide. The cool emotionless metallic click as the bullet slid into the chamber seemed to echo around the pumpkin patch.

Dr. Adriana Hart stared at the agent as he lowered his pistol to her forehead. "Please," she said as her voice caught in her throat. "Please just save him," Tears fell from her eyes as Poole looked at her silently.

From the edge of the SCP Murphy heard a crack like thunder and watched as crows flew up into the nighttime sky.

Dr. Adriana Hart's blood gleamed in the moonlight as it spread across the pumpkins and the surrounding field. Poole lifted her lifeless body and threw it over his shoulder and turned to the giant pumpkin, her son had finally reached the group. He blinked his eyes slowly and looked around, a gray pallor overtook his face as the nightmarish scene unfolded before him. He opened his mouth to scream but suddenly a large gloved hand clamped down over his face. Poole looked around at the surrounding creatures, he had taken off his sunglasses.

For what seemed like an eternity the field went silent and he stared at the red mist like eyes. Then with a grunt, he threw the doctor's body into the waiting maw of the pumpkin. His other blood-stained hand stayed tightly clenched across the boy's face, smearing red across his cheeks and lips. Poole leaned down and whispered for the kid to stay quiet as he withdrew his hand and motioned for him to follow. The creatures parted as they passed and Poole slowly sat down his backpack and picked up the kid, carrying him away from the blood-soaked field.

By the next morning, they walked out of the gates around the edge of the SCP and Poole sat him down on the ground by the gate. "Christ..." Murphy said as he looked at Poole who had long since replaced his glasses. Poole nodded and handed Murphy a small red detonator. Murphy looked at it and then at Poole, "Is this what I think it is?" Poole nodded again and pointed at the kid. "Make sure he goes to a good home yeah?" Murphy looked at the kid and then at Poole and walked over to him. Poole watched as he knelt and placed a hand on the kid's shoulder. "You ok son?" Murphy said as the bleary-eyed child looked up at him. He sniffled and nodded, a small sad smile coming across his face.

Then Murphy drove the blade of his tactical knife directly into the child's heart.

Poole watched, the only sign of his shock being the widening of his eyes, as the little boy twitched once and then let out a sigh. Murphy stood up and wiped his knife off, "I had my orders agent, just like you." Poole looked at Murphy and nodded as he turned and walked away. His hands drifted into his pocket and wrapped around a secondary detonator.

Two days later Poole was sitting in his room at Yellowstone when an alert popped up on his phone. Primary detonator detected within the blast radius, Poole looked at the alert and then at the detonator on his rooms only table. He walked over nonchalantly and picked it up. In one smooth motion, he flipped up the plastic button covering and pressed the button. Then Poole walked out of the room and headed towards the machine shop.

quickdraws were good, napalm was better.

CHAPTER 3 SCP-184 & SCP-106

Item #: SCP-184
Object Class: Euclid

Special Containment Procedures: SCP-184 is not to be contained in any structure. SCP-184 is to be attached to a high-power electromagnet at all times. Should the electromagnet fail, agents are to report to SCP-184's containment area and prevent access to all unauthorized personnel until the electromagnet is restored to power. The containment area for SCP-184 is currently configured to resemble a park with SCP-184 and its containment magnet disguised as statuary. Any and all visitors are to be monitored. Any structures affected by SCP-184 are to be demolished after review by [DATA EXPUNGED]. Final demolition approval or inclusion into SCP will also be determined by this body. No investigation is to be done into affected structures without approval and a rescue team on standby.

Description: SCP-184 is a small, smooth metallic object, 10 cm (4 in) tall and 10 cm (4 in) wide, in the shape of a dodecahedron. Each face of the figure has a circular hole in the center, and a small sphere is attached to each vertex. SCP-184 is made of an unknown, but highly magnetic, alloy about as hard as brass.

When inside an enclosed structure, SCP-184 expands the structure's inner dimensions without altering its outer dimensions. SCP-184 will increase the inner dimensions of any enclosed structure by several hundred meters each day, beginning one hour after entry into the structure. Initially, SCP-184 only extends the walls out, causing rooms to become much larger without adjusting the height of the room. This expansion continues until the original dimensions of the room have been tripled.

J. Poole : Agent of the Foundation

At this point, SCP-184 starts creating wholly new rooms. SCP-184 is apparently able to copy items from inside the structure, creating furnished rooms consistent with the rest of the structure. After a period of time, however, the expansion process appears to break down. For example, items will be made from inappropriate materials (glass books, a wooden microwave), rooms will be oddly-shaped, doors will open into blank walls, and hallways will be tiny or twist back around in long mazes. The new inside structures continue to be more and more odd, while the outside remains unchanged.

This behavior is most dramatically illustrated in homes; however, it has been observed in other instances, including a cardboard box. The changes do not go away with the removal of SCP-184, but no additional structures are created.

Addendum 184 - 1: Notes from Dr.

I don't think I need to stress the fact that this thing can NEVER be allowed into Site-19. We may need to look into different containment at some point, but for the time being, we will keep it in the open, immovable, and hidden.

Addendum 184 - 2: Locations of Interest

It is currently hypothesized that SCP-184 or an anomaly with a similar effect may be responsible for the creation of Locations of Interest such as Backdoor SoHo, and Chūgoku Cellar. Investigation into SCP-184 as a potential origin for these spaces is ongoing.

Addendum 184 – 38RB: Notes on recovery

SCP-184 was recovered in the Kowloon Walled City in June of ███████. Reports of the city's bizarre and explosive growth attracted Operatives, who soon learned of SCP-184, held in the possession of [DATA EXPUNGED]. After several police crackdowns, Mobile Task Force Zeta-9 was dispatched and recovered SCP-184 with minimal losses. The final effect of exposure to SCP-184 on both the City and inhabitants may never fully be understood due to the reckless actions of local law enforcement, which destroyed several affected sections of the city before Operatives could take action to prevent it. Interviews with residents yielded minimal information, with a communal "wall of silence" being the major response. A few documents indicated that SCP-184 could be brought into a home and allowed to affect the dwelling for 50 pounds sterling per half hour. These documents were unconfirmed by residents.

Addendum 184 – 38RB-s: Additional Documentation.

Personal Log of: Gordon Richards, member of Mobile team Zeta-9, the Mole Rats

Date: June 3rd, █████

Dispatched to the "Kowloon Walled City" to recover an object and document anything affected by it. I have never seen such a horrible place. The filth is everywhere, whole walls and even structures made of garbage. If you crack your suit for even a second, you get flooded by the smell of smoke, cooking, sweat, machine oil and excrement. Henry fell into a pit used as a sewer on the ground level after breaking through a trash walkway. He was fine, the suit was just filthy, but he threw up and had to be removed. I'm not sure if he's going to work out. Everyone here avoids us like the plague, or darts out to throw trash or insults. They are a tribe, and a territorial one at that. The sheer crush of humanity is intimidating, and I'm glad I have the suit between me and them. The object is supposed to be somewhere in the core of this mass, but getting there is going to be tricky.

Date: June 4th,

███

Local law enforcement led by Agents did a bunch of raids last night. Cleared people out of some of the areas we need to go in, but there are so many people here it's hard to notice any difference. Yesterday's recon helped uncover a couple "homes" affected by this thing. They don't look like much, the same squalid homes as everyone else, but they are too big inside. It's an odd feeling, standing with your hand on the wall, and knowing that by all rights you should be six feet outside the structure, in mid-air. Henry is better today, but seems really jumpy. Lev took him aside and talked to him last night, and I hope it's helped. I'm getting worried about him. Caught him muttering to himself over the radio today. Told him to knock it off, but didn't report it, maybe I should have. I think I'm going to ask for him to be put on a different unit after this.

Deep recon this evening, we're splitting up to try and hunt down where they are storing this thing. Lev and I pulled the short stick and have to hike it around the sewer system. Honestly, it can't be any worse than topside; at least I won't have to keep seeing the blank, empty faces of these people.

Date: June 6th, ███

Henry is dead. We didn't get back until early this morning; we'd been off the radio for several hours because of all the interference. It seems areas affected by this thing screw with radio waves pretty bad. The sewer was a nightmare, but no sign of alteration by the item. When we came back up, Paul gave me the news. Henry and Paul were exploring near the center of the city when they got attacked. A mob of people swarmed them and dragged Henry off. Paul was hurt and his suit was badly damaged, and he had to leave for medical attention. Henry was screaming over the radio for a while, and then it cut off. Paul and a couple other Mole Rats charged in with some agents to recover Henry, but after a few minutes,

Henry came back on the radio.

His receiver was broken, but he could still broadcast. One of the Agents was recording, and he played it back to Lev and I, to see if any of it made sense to us. It didn't. He was rambling and sounded like he was hurt. Kept talking about the endless heart of the city, the hell of glass, just crazy stuff. Paul and the rescue team kept trying to find him, but suddenly his radio cut out again.

Henry came tearing down one of those tiny halls, helmet off and screaming like a mad man. He ran right by Paul and smashed an Agent into a wall on his way by. He slammed into a dead end and just exploded through it, right out of the building. He fell six stories onto some metal junk. It took an hour to get his body untangled. We're done screwing around here. Agent Parks, Lev and me are rounding up what amounts to the city elders, and we're getting to the damn bottom of this.

Date: June 7th, █████

Interrogation went well. Agent Parks asked the questions, we provided what he called "negative consequences for non-cooperation". The first guy, some Triad punk, didn't want to talk. Two broken legs later, and he was a lot more open. Said the thing was called "The Builder", and nobody knew when it first came to the city. He never had anything to do with it, just helped stand guard outside rooms where it was working. He said that was all he knew, and that we had to talk to one of the elders, Long-Wen, if we wanted it. He apologized for Henry's death, said it was just the way of things. I broke his jaw in three places.

Long-Wen may be the oldest-looking man I've ever seen, and with a will like iron. He just took everything we dished out, and didn't say a word. Parks said that the next stop was his wife and grandkids, and that got him talking. Told us it was kept in one of the oldest parts of the city, some old temple. It had grown, and made wonderful things, but only the worthy could look upon it and not be overwhelmed by it. He said Henry was

J. Poole : Agent of the Foundation

shown the wonders, in the hopes that he would be able to convince us to not take The Builder, but that he was not worthy, and was broken.

We made him show us where they keep it. Long-Wen said it wouldn't do any good, that it was buried too deep. They moved it deep inside when they first caught wind of the Agents; he said we'd never get it back. We're doing Deep Work tomorrow, and we're not coming out without it.

Date: June 10th, ████

Been out for a while. This place is amazing. At first, it was just a temple that was too big inside, neat but nothing new. Then we went in deeper. Whole rooms, altars, everything re-created and rearranged by this thing. It's like someone built twelve whole temples inside this one tiny structure. Agent Parks set up a recall point in the main hall with some other Agents to make sure nobody sneaks up on us. We suited up and went to work. It started getting odd after hour six. Lots of hallways, not as many rooms. Then, eighty-three rooms all connected by those sliding doors, each with a tiny Buddha in the center of the floor, and nothing else. Lev grabbed a few for samples. We knew things were getting odd when we came to a perfect reproduction of the first altar room, but appearing to be made of one solid mass of wood.

Thing was beautiful and totally seamless, and not a single tool mark on anything. Paul found some documents, and we scanned them back to Parks. He said they were about the object; apparently they're calling it SCP-184 now. Parks said it talks about how they moved 184 deeper each time it made a new area. They thought it was some gift from God or something. Used it to expand rooms, if people would donate to the temple, or at least to the gangs that controlled it at the time.

I've never been in a place like this. It's getting harder to maneuver. The halls are starting to get strange, they go up at funny angles, and the last few rooms have been tiny. By Lev's count, we should be twenty feet above the roof of this whole

73

Steven L. Stamm

city by now.

Date: June 12th(?), █████

I'm getting sick of this place. Came to a branch yesterday, had to split the team. I drew the "up" hallway, and set out. Not sure how long I've been climbing. The halls aren't regular anymore; they wave in and out, like a frozen earthquake. Everything seems to be made of stone here. Managed to squeeze into a side room to catch my breath, once I looked around, I saw everything was made of jade. It was all colored right, and had the right texture, but it was jade. Bed, chairs, table, books, everything. I sat on the bed for two hours and didn't think. I got up and smashed the jade lamp that was probably worth more than my life, and left.

I'm not feeling well. I feel really disconnected here, like an astronaut or something. It's not like other areas I've been in. Never felt so alone. I'm fine, I know that. It's Henry dying, the whole rotten city outside, and me being alone and able to think too much. Rats are tested for mental stability, and I passed with flying colors. It's just my nerves. I'm sitting on a chair made of thousands of tiny dragon statues, writing on a table made of super-dense paper, and I am fine.

Date: June (?)

I've been out too long. Food low. Water low. Not out yet, but getting there. Hearing things. Keep thinking I hear voices. Been climbing for days. Saw light today. At the end of a side-hall, bright yellow light. I climbed into the hall and ran. Smashed through the door, and it was a room. Millions of candles, all lit, but just another room. Pulled off my helmet, smashed the candles with it. Broke my lenses, neck seal, radio. Didn't care. Sat and cried for hours. Dropped a pick down the shaft today, never heard it hit bottom. Almost jumped to go get it, but stopped. Got to find this thing. Going to smash it to bits. Stomp it. Crush it.

74

J. Poole : Agent of the Foundation
Date: June (?)
Food out. Suit can't make any more water. Saw a hall with ten thousand doors. Ran down it, smashed a bunch, then kept climbing. Lost my boots. Floor looked like carpet. Made of super-sharp stone. Cut suit to ribbons. Feet too. Blood all over the shaft. Hope it appreciates it. Going to crush this thing. Feel it shatter in my hand. Hate this place. Keep hearing Henry. Keep telling him he's dead. Won't listen.

Date: (?)
Top of shaft. Hall to forever. Lights everywhere. Going to kill the heart.

Date: (?)
Hell is Heaven
Heaven is Hell
Life is Wonderful

Notes: Gordon Richards went missing during the recovery of SCP-184, presumed KIA. SCP-184 recovered by Team Zeta-9. Journal recovered in rubble left from destruction of SCP-184 affected temple.

==

Item #: SCP-106

Object Class: Keter

Special Containment Procedures:

No physical interaction with SCP-106 is allowed at any time. All physical interaction must be approved by no less than a two-thirds vote from O5-Command, and may only extend to testing situations. All staff (Research, Security, Class D, etc.) are to remain at least twenty meters away from the containment cell at all times, except for mandated maintenance and re-evaluation checks.

Containment cell must be held suspended in a secondary cell, the walls of which must be at least thirty meters distant from the outer walls of the first or "primary" cell. The secondary cell is to remain under total observation at all times, and be both illuminated and clear of any and all debris. Any items, movement, or non-normal activity noted within the secondary cell will result in a full site lock-down. Lock-down will be maintained until a "situation normal" dispatch is issued by Site Command.

Any corrosion observed on the primary cell, secondary cell, staff members, or other site locations within two hundred meters of SCP-106 are to be reported to Site Security immediately. Any objects or personnel lost to SCP-106 are to be deemed missing/KIA. No recovery attempts are to be made under any circumstances.

Note: SCP-106 does not have a "docile" state. Any reduction in activity or increased compliance from SCP-106 is to be deemed a luring tactic immediately preceding an aggressive action, and treated as such.

NOTE: SCP DISCONTINUED DUE TO ESCAPE PERCENTAGE

No physical interaction with SCP-106 is allowed at any time. All physical interaction must be approved by no less than a two-thirds vote from O5-Command, and may only extend to testing situations. All staff (Research, Security, Class D, etc.) are to remain at least thirty meters away from the containment cell at all times, except under direct order from Site Command.

SCP-106 is to be kept within a sealed container, comprised of sixteen layers of lead-lined steel, each separated by no less than 18cm of open space aside from minimal support struts. Said container is to be kept suspended by a "continuous current" system within a fluid medium. This medium is to be replaced in 48 hour cycles, and constantly monitored for any "corrosion" intrusion.

Any corrosion observed on any containment cell surfaces, staff members, or other site locations within two hundred meters of SCP-106 are to be reported to Site Security immediately. Any objects or personnel lost to SCP-106 are to be deemed missing/KIA. No recovery attempts are to be made under any circumstances.

SCP-106 does not have a "docile" state. Any reduction in activity or increased compliance from SCP-106 is to be deemed a luring tactic immediately preceding an aggressive action, and treated as such.

Note: Observation of SCP-106 has shown a slight "resistance" when passing through lead or other similar metals. The thickness of the material appears to make no difference. In addition, multiple layers of thin material appear to "slow" SCP-106, forcing it to enter and re-emerge multiple times. Fluids also appear to temporarily "confuse" SCP-106.

NOTE: SCP DISCONTINUED DUE TO MULTIPLE SURFACE BREACHES. AGITATION SYSTEM CONTINUED TO DISPERSE CORROSION DURING BREACH EVENT, RESULTING IN MULTIPLE BREACHES AND FULL CONTAINMENT FAILURE
REVISION 11-8

No physical interaction with SCP-106 is allowed at any time. All physical interaction must be approved by no less than a two-thirds vote from O5-Command. Any such interaction must be undertaken in AR-II maximum security sites, after a general non-essential staff evacuation. All staff (Research, Security, Class D, etc.) are to remain at least sixty meters away from the containment cell at all times, except in the event of breach events.

SCP-106 is to be contained in a sealed container, comprised of lead-lined steel. The container will be sealed within forty layers of identical material, each layer separated by no less than 36cm of empty space. Support struts between layers are to be randomly spaced. Container is to remain suspended no less than 60cm from any surface by ELO-IID electromagnetic supports.

Secondary containment area is to be comprised of sixteen spherical "cells", each filled with various fluids and a random assembly of surfaces and supports. Secondary containment is to be fitted with light systems, capable of flooding the entire assembly with no less than 80,000 lumens of light instantly with no direct human involvement. Both containment areas are to remain under 24 hour surveillance.

Any corrosion observed on any containment cell surfaces, staff members, or other site locations within two hundred meters of SCP-106 are to be reported to Site Security immediately. Any objects or personnel lost to SCP-106 are to be deemed missing/KIA. No recovery attempts are to be made under any circumstances.

Note: Continued research and observation have shown that, when faced with highly complex/random assemblies of structures, SCP-106 can be "confused", showing a marked delay on entry and exit from said structure. SCP-106 has also shown an aversion to direct, sudden light. This is not manifested in any form of physical damage, but a rapid exit in to the "pocket dimension" generated on solid surfaces.

These observations, along with those of lead-aversion and liquid confusion, have reduced the general escape incidents by 43%. The "primary" cells have also been effective in recovery incidents requiring Recall Protocol ███ -███ -█. Observation is ongoing.

Description: SCP-106 appears to be an elderly humanoid, with a general appearance of advanced decomposition. This appearance may vary, but the "rotting" quality is observed in all forms. SCP-106 is not exceptionally agile, and will remain motionless for days at a time, waiting for prey. SCP-106 is also capable of scaling any vertical surface and can remain suspended upside down indefinitely. When attacking, SCP-106 will attempt to incapacitate prey by damaging major organs, muscle groups, or tendons, then pull disabled prey into its pocket dimension. SCP-106 appears to prefer human prey items in the 10-25 years of age bracket.

SCP-106 causes a "corrosion" effect in all solid matter it touches, engaging a physical breakdown in materials several seconds after contact. This is observed as rusting, rotting, and cracking of materials, and the creation of a black, mucus-like substance similar to the material coating SCP-106. This effect is particularly detrimental to living tissues, and is assumed to be a "pre-digestion" action. Corrosion continues for six hours after contact, after which the effect appears to "burn out". SCP-106 is capable of passing through solid matter, leaving behind a large patch of its corrosive mucus. SCP-106 is able to "vanish" inside solid matter, entering what is assumed to be a form of "pocket dimension". SCP-106 is then able to exit this dimension from any point connected to the initial entry point (examples: "entering" the inner wall of a room, and "exiting" the outer wall. Entering a wall, and exiting from the ceiling). It is unknown if this is the point of origin for SCP-106, or a simple "lair" created by SCP-106.
Limited observation of this "pocket dimension" has shown it to be comprised mostly of halls and rooms, with [DATA EXPUNGED] entry. This activity can continue for days, with some subjected individuals being released for the express purpose of hunting, recapture, [DATA EXPUNGED].

Addendum:

SCP Review Notes:
Due to the exceedingly difficult-to-contain nature of SCP-106, SCP is to be reviewed every three months or during a post-breach incident. Physical restraints are impossible, and direct physical damage appears to have no effect on SCP-106. Current SCP, as of ███/██/███, revolves around basic observation and immediate response. Previous, more proactive special containment procedures have been recalled due to the events of breaches ███, ███, ███, █, and ████.

Notes on behavior:
SCP-106 appears to go through long periods of "dormancy", in which it will remain completely motionless for up to three months. The cause for this is unknown; however, it has been shown that this appears to be used as a "lulling" tactic. SCP-106 will emerge from this state in a very agitated state, and will attack and abduct staff and cause gross damage to its containment cell and the site at large. Recall Protocol [DATA EXPUNGED].
SCP-106 appears to hunt and attack based on desire, not hunger. SCP-106 will attack and collect multiple prey items during a hunting behavior event, keeping many "alive" in the pocket dimension for extended periods of time. SCP-106 has no determinable "limit", and appears to collect a random number of prey items during an event.
The inner dimension accessed by SCP-106 appears to be only accessible by SCP-106. Recording and transmission devices have been shown to still operate inside this dimension, though recordings and transmissions are very degraded. It appears that SCP-106 will "play" with captured prey, and appears to have full control of time, space, and perception inside this dimension. SCP-106 appears [DATA EXPUNGED].
Recall Protocol ███-███-█:
In the event of a breach event by SCP-106, a human within the

10-25 years of age bracket will be prepped for recall, with the compromised containment cell being replaced and restored for use. When the cell is ready, the lure subject will be injured, preferably via the breakage of a long bone, such as the femur, or the severing of a major tendon, such as the Achilles Tendon. Lure subject will then be placed in the prepped cell, and the sound emitted by said subject will be transmitted over the site public address system.

THE CHAOS INSURGENCY

Overview: The Chaos Insurgency is a splinter group of the Foundation, created by a rogue cell that went A.W.O.L. with several SCP objects in 1924. Since then, the Insurgency has become a major player on the world stage, using the anomalies that it obtains for its own benefit and to consolidate its global power base. The Insurgency not only deals in anomalies, but also in weapons running and intelligence gathering.

It makes use of authoritarian regimes in poor and developing countries, often using their populations in the same manner as the Foundation does D-Class personnel. It helps to maintain the extreme poverty and war that is suffered by these countries, so that it can continue its radical experimentation, easy conscription of forces, and lucrative business deals with various opposing factions.

Most of the anomalous objects possessed by the Insurgency are unknown. Among the most notable items are the "Staff of Hermes", an item capable of warping the physical and chemical properties of any matter it touches, and the "Bell of Entropy", an object that can cause a variety of destructive effects depending on where it is struck. Both of these objects were originally obtained at no small cost by the Foundation, and were stolen by the original founders of the Insurgency. The SCP objects and other anomalies stolen from the Foundation typically possess high potential for direct utility, but the Insurgency has also made use of anomalies with less direct applications, such as SCP-884.

The main base of operations of the Insurgency is unknown, as are its current leaders. This organization is directly antagonistic to the Foundation, using deadly force to attempt to prevent Foundation containment of multiple anomalies. The Foundation has also been infiltrated by agents of the Insurgency in the past, resulting in the loss of valuable scientific data, theft of a number of anomalies, and deaths of personnel. Personnel are made to be aware of possible raids, terrorist action, and spies from the Insurgency, and are to notify their superiors about any activities from fellow personnel fitting the Insurgency behavioral profile.

===

Caleb turned the corner and fell to his knees. The … thing, was fucking hunting him. He looked at the walls of the office he had run into and wheezed out a profanity. Of course, the room would be entirely made from 10-99 expense reports. He slowly moved into the room, carefully reaching out with his hands into the all-consuming darkness around him. The glow stick hanging around his neck gave off a small sickly green chemical glow.

It had been, by his reckoning, over two weeks since the agent had arrived. Agent Becker had walked in with a badge from one of those alphabet government organizations and a pompous swagger; he had demanded to see the basement. When he had walked past Caleb's cubicle he had smiled at the agent. However, once he had passed however Caleb had thrown open his desk drawer and pulled out his bug out bag and ran for the exits. Only when he got there he found that the doors had been chained shut with a heavy padlocked chain.

J. Poole : Agent of the Foundation

That was when the blue gas had started to seep out of the vents along the floorboards. But Caleb was smart and he had planned for things like this. As he pulled on his army surplus gas mask and ran for the stairs he grinned like a madman. He thought about all his dumbass coworkers who were about to bite the dust thanks to what was obviously a terrorist attack. He ran up the stairs and was shocked to find that the door to the roof was locked. He slammed his back against the door and slumped against the door frame and closed his eyes and waited for his air to run out. He thought how he would look to all the mourners when they came by to witness the site of this attack, maybe they would even make a poster of him.

He waited for the air canister in his mask to run out and for the gas to finally reach him. But, by the time the canister ran dry the blue gas was nowhere to be seen. Caleb crept to the edge of the stairway's railing and looked down, it looked like a blue fog had settled below the landing below him. He stared at it for a second and then squatted against a nearby wall. He slid his bag off his shoulder and onto the ground and unzipped it. He had enough rations to last for a month if he needed them, and so he waited.

After three days of waiting, Caleb was finally able to descend the stairs, and when he did he found something he wasn't expecting. The stairs went farther down than before, going deeper and deeper into seemingly infinite darkness. After reaching what should have been the first floor he paused. His hand gripped the door and pushed it open slowly. He knew the front door was just three yards in front of him and he could make it there in five seconds if he sprinted, two if he tossed the bag. He took a deep breath and pushed the door open with his shoulder and ran.

Almost instantly he skidded to a stop. He looked

around wildly and realized he was in a hallway that terminated in a single wooden door. Thick black mucus dripped in sheets from every wall. The smell hit him like a physical force and reminded Caleb of the slaughterhouse he worked in as a teenager. The pungent odor was like a mixture of piss and shit, the smells of a sudden and brutal death. He slowly moved into the hallway muttering curses in a whisper as he passed the blackened walls.

Out of the corner of his eye, in that small space on the edge of your vision where you sometimes think you see someone standing behind you who isn't really there; he saw something move across the ceiling. He whirled around looking for whatever was moving in the shadows. This caused him to slip and fall, the mucus coating his legs and making it hard to gain purchase. As he flailed on the ground his eyes were drawn to the naked light bulb above him. It's monotone hum of quiet electrical bliss calming him.

That was when he saw the hand emerge from the mass of viscous material, like a person rising from the water. A hand covered in skin the color of parchment and dotted with oozing pustules grasped the light. Caleb felt his mouth go dry and his whole body go still as if controlled by an ancient primal instinct. The fluorescent light bulb creaked as the creature began to surge forth.

Its body was that of an aged man with gaunt features. Skin was missing in rotted chunks across its body and its necrotic eyes were illuminated by an inhuman yellow glow. Where the skin was missing bloody muscles and tendons surged and twisted. In some parts, white masses of wriggling maggots seemed to almost swim through the creature's flesh. Caleb watched in abject horror as the thing turned it's face towards him and dropped its skinless jaw in a ghoulish inhuman grin. Its tongue slid out from between a gap in its rotten yellow teeth and seemed to elongate towards Caleb. "Oh shit," He said he began to scramble for the door. With a renewed vigor he scraped his way to the door and pushed it open, throwing himself to the other side.

Caleb turned around and watched as the creature's head bent at an impossible angle and stared at him. Then, with a sound like a hand snapping a bundle of twigs, the creature crushed the light. Leaving only its glowing eyes to shine in the darkness as Caleb slammed the door shut. With a shuddering sigh, he slid to the ground with his back to the door and stared at his surroundings. Hallways split off from this room in countless directions. Hundreds of doors and openings seemed to surround him in a gigantic sphere splitting off into infinite paths. With a whimper, Caleb pulled out a chemical light stick and cracked it and looped it over his neck.

Suddenly the strap of his bag tightened around his body and felt like it was being pulled through the wall. Caleb let out a screech and slipped out of the strap as the bag vanished into the black slime that coated the door. He stared at the growing spot and let out a mouse-like squeak when he saw a rotting hand begin to reach through. Caleb hauled himself to his feet and backed away quickly as the spot grew, then he turned and ran down the nearest hall.

Now he was in a room made out of paperwork and his last light was dying. Caleb looked around in abject horror as he realized there was no exit. Tears formed in his eyes as he moved to the center of the room, the thing couldn't get him there. He stared at the door, the creatures scraping gait was getting louder every second.

Sccccccchhhhhhh.....
klunk......sssssssccccccchhhhhh........klunk

Then it went silent.

Caleb stared at the door frame and felt a sob catch in his throat. "FUCKING DO IT!!" He screamed in an animalistic fury at the empty hallway. That was when he felt the hand around his ankle tighten.

...

"And as such we must ensure that the security of the captured SCP remains intact", The presenter was droning on and on for what seemed like an endless eternity. Poole couldn't help but feel his hatred for the person presenting burning hotter with each syllable. "Agent Poole," a voice whispered making Poole start to turn around. "Keep looking ahead Agent," The voice was gruff and harsh. Each letter dripped authority and gravitas with its intonation. The speaker was someone whom Poole had never actually seen in person but one everybody knew. It was a member of the O-5 council.

"Agent," The councilperson said as he leaned forward. "You are aware of the Chaos insurgency." It was a statement, one which caused shivers to go down Poole's back. The Chaos insurgency was a group he was not only familiar with but one he despised. "It has come to our attention that they have managed to turn one of our agents..." Poole narrowed his eyes and nodded, "So you need me to exterminate the rogue agent?" "Too late for that I am afraid," the sound of a match striking and the heady scent of tobacco drifted through the air as the O-5 lit a cigarette. "He committed suicide as a martyr for their cause over two weeks ago. He released SCP-106 and SCP-184 by use of a transdimensional gateway." Poole raised an eyebrow and shifted slightly. "How in the hell did he manage that?" The O-5 agent let out a steady smoke-filled breath. "It would seem he had lodged two anomalous passages within his person. Upon activation, the

J. Poole : Agent of the Foundation
security cameras show his body exploding from within and expelling both SCPs. It was rather gruesome and not something we would recommend viewing."

"What is the mission then, secure and protect?" Poole said as he stood up and buttoned his suit. "Not exactly, more something along the lines of finding the SCP's and contain them if possible, but also they left a message." Poole froze, his hand stopping on his lowest button. "It said to send you, by name." Poole swore softly and finished buttoning up his suit, "who else knows about this?" The agent sniffed and coughed, "The rest of the council and Dr.Bright; he is being flown in for a special consult on this matter. I would suggest we focus on this later. Your car is waiting for you"

Poole rode in silence on the long drive from Yellowstone to the office building. The benefit of being a one-man MTF meant that you were often left alone with your thoughts. Poole was relishing this opportunity as he mulled over the words the O-5 operative had told him. The Chaos insurgency was involved in this and that was never good. In fact, for him at least, it was particularly bad as they had been trying to kill him for some time. What's more, is they were bringing in Dr.Bright, Poole had worked with him before (or at least copies of him). But Bright was a madman and a lunatic, they only brought him onto projects where his vessel could afford to die.

It had been a long night the last time he had tangled with the insurgency and the scars the fight had left were more psychological than physical. He shivered at the thought of going up against them again. Poole pulled the modified 1911 from its holster again and slid back the slide to check the chamber again. He knew that if he was going to survive what came next he was going to need his wits about him. After ensuring his pistol was in prime operating condition he took a deep breath and just concentrated on the drive. This was not going to be a fun trip.

By the time he reached the office building the foundation had set up a surrounding barrier to keep the onlookers out. Still, he decided to wait until nightfall, just to be sure nobody saw him. By the time he decided to go in the only person watching was a homeless man who had been begging for change on the street corner. "Name?" The agent said as Poole pulled up to the gate. "J. Poole, O-5 designation" the agent snapped to attention and waved him forward, " You will want to talk with doctor Graham sir."

Dr. Graham was a man of Indian descent and stood in the center of the building's parking lot. His eyes searching the windows of the building for something as he raised his cigarette to his lips. Poole approached as he drew a drag on the smoke, illuminating and deepening the valleys and peaks of his face. "A pleasure to see you again agent." Poole nodded as he stood next to Graham," Hard to believe they are sending me into this again." Graham nodded and took another draw," You have the experience and the history for dealing with this. As well as... the skill set." Poole raised an eyebrow, "Indeed."

Graham sighed and tossed the stub of his cigarette on the ground, grinding out the glowing embers with the heel of his foot. "You know Poole, there was a time I would have liked to see you do this kind of thing." Poole smiled darkly, "you were younger then." Graham let out a soft chuckle, "And stupider too... but now I am scared of what may happen if we lose you." Poole nodded at this and patted his side, "I made a promise to work for the foundation." Graham shook his head and stared at the building again, "A promise only goes so far Poole, I know what they did to you last time." "That was a long time ago." Poole stepped forward and looked at the building. Graham shrugged and motioned to a nearby soldier.

"Make sure anything that comes out of there besides this man is shredded." He said, his voice cold and calculating. "Yes sir," The young man saluted and ran back to his post. "They really aren't anything like they used to be," Poole said as he watched the soldier take position behind a machine gun. Graham seemed to think for a moment and then turned towards the building, "We don't need them to be."

Poole's hand rested on the handle for the front door, it was cold to the touch. In his ear, the radio squeaked as Graham's voice came over the air. "Agent Poole, you are good to go. eeshvar tumhaaree madad kare." Poole nodded and ripped the door open, stepping fearlessly into the cavernous first floor of the building. His footsteps echoed around him as he slowly moved forward into the lobby. The clack of the front door locking shut as it swung closed behind him sounded like a gunshot in the empty room. "Graham?" Poole said as he looked around, the marble floor and wood walls stretched into the darkness. No reply. "Shit", Poole pulled his pistol free and turned on its tactical light.

He moved deeper into the lobby and came to a wooden doorway, black sludge seeped around the edges. Poole looked at the door for a moment and then with a steady hand he pushed the door open. Inside a hallway with a single light bulb stretched across to a red door. Slowly Poole stepped forward into the shadowy corridor. His feet slid along slightly with each step and he began to notice that every inch of the hallway was coated in thick black goo. He had made it halfway across when he heard the sound of scraping wood behind him.

Poole spun in place and raised his pistol only for it to illuminate the door behind him. It was closed, and there were three deep gashes carved into the wood. Poole began to slowly back towards the door that was now behind him. As he neared it he noticed something moving on the ceiling, something just out of his line of sight. Crawling along like a skittering beetle on the edge of his vision. Poole placed a hand behind him and felt it close around the handle of the red door.

That was when he noticed it, a bump was forming in the ceiling next to the light. Poole slowly turned the door handle as he watched an arm slowly slide through the ooze. With a sickening thud, a human arm hit the ground, parts of it missing as if having been gnawed on. Blood oozed from where it had been ripped off of the body and the marrow of the bone jutted forward like a white fibrous feather. Poole moved backward through the door and pulled it shut.

He turned around and froze. Before him, the floor terminated at a 90-degree angle plunging downwards into nothingness. Doors and walls within the abyss before him jutted randomly in directions impossible to understand. Hallways seemed to spiral into one another creating impossible peaks and doors piled upon one another opening and closing rapidly as if a mountain composed of the madness of one MC Escher. They seemed to have heights that stretched to some dark heavens and roots which disappeared from sight. The cacophony as unseen telephones rang in the distance and the audible groan of alien cyclopean architecture seemed to surround him. And from every crevice poured a constant stream of thick black fluid. From seemingly nowhere and everywhere at once a light shone, illuminating the alien landscape before him.

For a moment his mind felt like it was on fire. Then, cautiously, he peered over the edge of where the floor dropped off. Below him, the floor didn't disappear so much as make a ninety-degree turn downwards. As he looked down he could see a door looking back at him. The fall had to be at least fifty or sixty feet, so he jumped. He fell quickly and the air rushed by his ears as he watched the door rapidly approach him. As neared the door it swung open and he found himself flying forwards into a room full of an infinite number of cubicles and ringing phones.

Suddenly, and with a sickening jolt, gravity shifted and he found himself flying forward instead of downward. With a cry and a roll, Poole managed to slow himself. As he skidded to a stop he was able to take possession of his surroundings. The room stretched into the distance and everywhere he looked cubicles sat in rows upon rows. Each one held a ringing phone, and from the receivers poured more of the foul-smelling black liquid.

Poole watched as the door he had fallen through slammed shut and seemed to dissolve into the wall. Then he heard it, a steady scraping noise. It was coming from one of the aisles around him and Poole slowly began to try to orient himself towards the sound. Like a cat searching for a mouse, Poole moved in from cubicle to cubicle, slowly searching for the source of the noise. Eventually, he came across an aisle where the fluorescent lights didn't shine so brightly.

At the end of this aisle stood a figure, cloaked in shadow but slowly moving towards him. Poole shouted at the thing to stop moving and identify itself. It paused for a moment and moved into a nearby cubicle. Poole rushed forward and rounded the corner, but the thing was gone. That was when he heard the scraping noise again, directly behind him.

Poole turned with a cry and aimed his pistol towards the source of the noise. The bright light of his piece illuminated a horribly emaciated creature. It's lower half seemed to be skinless and the muscle mass and tendons moved freely, each twitch eliciting a mixture of wriggling maggots and black fluid. Its torso was peeled back and held open by steel hooks, its organs being branded with the sigil of the Chaos insurgency. With each wheezing breath, a putrid smell seemed to come from its decomposing lungs. But this all could have been ignored if not for the creature's face. Its skinless jaw stretched disgustedly, making the long black tongue which hung between its teeth comical in a macabre sort of way. With each huff of exertion, the creature coughed up black bile and long white worms. Its eyes were obviously decomposing but still shifted blindly in their sockets, casting a sickly yellow glow.

And yet, as impossible as it seems, it let out a neolithic cry and sucker-punched Poole in the side of his chest. Sending him flying through the cubicles with a sickening crack or breaking bone and the searing pain of a punctured lung. Poole coughed as the thing began to shuffle forward, blood-splattered his lips. He raised his pistol and began to fire at the advancing monster. Bullets ripped through the flesh of the otherworldly horror as it advanced, doing nothing to slow its movements.

Poole screamed in anger as his pistol clicked empty. With a howl of effort, he kicked at the advancing creature. With an almost lazy swipe, the creature smacked his leg to the side, snapping his femur with a loud explosive crack. This sent Poole spiraling across the room into more cubicles. The creature turned and advanced towards Poole slowly, its tongue probing the air before it. Poole watched as the creature reached him and it's tongue slowly slid across his face.

The thing bent down and moved closer to him, ignoring his steely-eyed gaze. Ignoring his eyes.

Poole felt fear start to take hold in his gut. Like a heavyweight that held him down, Poole felt his body start to sag. The tongue slowly began to circle his neck and he felt hands grasp his head. His world began to go dark and his mind began to drift.

J. Poole : Agent of the Foundation

Then in that darkness between life and death, a spark was lit. Not one of hope or a good memory. But a spark of pure unbridled rage at the audacity this thing had to try and kill him.

Poole's eyes flew open and he grabbed the tongue with both hands and with a primal roar he sunk his teeth into it. He tossed his head like a mad dog until the tongue ripped loose from the creature's maw and the beast let out a blood-curdling scream. It scrambled across the ground trying to get away from him but Poole was angry. In a frantic scramble, he grabbed the creature by the ankle and pulled his body on top of it, turning it over in the process. With a grunt, he slammed his head into its skull, again and again, his blood and its black bile mixing on the floor. With a scream, he drove his thumb into its eyes and tore the ocular muscles from their sockets. The pathetic thing wailed in horror as he sat up and with a mad cackle drove his fist into its chest, ripping apart the sigil.

A blinding light burst into being around Poole and he found himself laying in the hallway of a clean and well-kept office building. The carpet felt fantastic under his beaten and broken body. But the bright lights hurt his eyes. With a groan, he turned his head searching for the SCP, but he couldn't see anything. Nearby he noticed a window looking out onto a blue sky, outside he could almost make out the sound of traffic and the foundation soldiers. He could have fallen asleep except for one thing, someone was humming in the conference room next to him.

With a groan, he hauled himself to his feet and leaned against the wall. Slowly he shuffled forward and, leaning on the door itself, he swung into the conference room.

The room was moderately sized for a conference room. Its walls were a cool corporate gray and a long oak table squatted in the center. At the head of the table sat an elderly man in a well-pressed suit. His face was ridged with the lines of age and in his gnarled hands, he held the second SCP. His demeanor was almost like that of a grandfather, save for his eyes. Those terrible eyes seemed to belong to another face, of a much younger and much crueler persuasion. He smiled as Poole entered the room.

"Herr agent," the man said as he nodded his head. "Jetzt treffen wir uns wieder," his smile widened and grew cold as Poole placed a supporting hand onto the top of the desk in front of him. Poole spat out a glouble of blood and a tooth, "How the fuck are you alive?" The old man stood up, shaking slightly as he straightened. "Mein Freund, surely you know I would not let our game rest? You couldn't have expected this to simply stop, after all these years?" Poole grimaced and slid slightly as he adjusted his weight on the table.

"I had hoped you had died." The man's face immediately turned to a glowering frown. "No, I don't think I could die knowing you went through all that trouble for me. There were children on that Luftschiff, women, and families. You killed them all just to kill me." Poole gritted his teeth and grinned, "Oh the fucking humanity, you did so much worse, Good doctor." The old man reeled back as if he had been physically slapped, his face contorting into a mask of rage. "HOW DARE YOU! I did what was necessary to make use of those poor wretches. I fixed god's mistakes and I made men out of beasts." Poole glared at the old man and spit, "you killed thousands." "You. Killed. My. Family." He roared, his fist slamming into the table for emphasis. Poole looked at him, his expression cold and heartless, "They died like dogs."

The old man's eyes gleamed with bitter hate and tossed the SCP to Poole. With a lurch, he slid off the table and caught it in his hand. "Herr agent be warned that our game now begins again. But I have new allies, my old friend. And we have a message for you and your 'foundation'." The old man bent down with a groan and whispered in Poole's ear.

Die alten Götter sind auferstanden, sie sind hier. hörst du sie klopfen

With that, he stood up and smiled at Poole. Then he drew back his leg and kicked Poole's nose hard enough to illicit a sickening crack. With a whispered word his very form dissolved into a black mist. Poole screamed in rage as the blood began to pour from his nose, his fingers tearing at the carpet where the old man had stood. Eventually, he would pass out and drift into a dreamless sleep.

Two days later...

Poole woke up with a start and stared around himself at the medical bay. After a few moments, he noticed the plain-clothed young man with sandy blond hair and a small impish nose. He was wearing a small ruby-red gem around his neck. "Poole." the young man said. "Dr.Bright," Poole grunted, his mouth was wired shut. "Forty-nine lacerations, three broken ribs with one punctured lung. Fourteen stab wounds and a broken femur." Bright said with the wave of a hand. "And a broken nose." Poole said as his eyes narrowed, "the hell are you doing here Bright?" Dr.Bright leaned back and regarded agent Poole through his glasses.

"What happened in there, Poole? Because the O-5 council called me specifically and diverted my flight to Yellowstone instead of our original meeting place." Poole looked at Dr.Bright and let out a sigh, "What do you know about the Thule society?"

EPILOUGE

Dr.Bright sat at his desk and watched agent Poole's vital signs on a small green handheld. Those fucking animals had almost killed him. Bright connected with Poole , after all he knew what it was like to be.... this way. They had worked together before; Poole was also probably the only one besides Graham who tolerated his antics. Shit, Poole even understood why he did what he did in those brief spurts of madness, he even coined the phrase 'letting of the psychological steam'. Dr. Bright let out a bone rattling too old for the body that made it and sat down his coffee mug and the handheld. He pinched the bridge of his nose between his thumb and fore finger and rubbed.

Poole would make a full recovery,no doubt about that. Brights hands lingered on the necklace around his neck. But what if next time he wouldn't?

They needed some insurance.

SCP-963

Item #: SCP-963

Object Class: Euclid

Special Containment Procedures: SCP-963-1 is to be given into the care of a current D level operative, as well as personnel classified as Dr. Bright's assistant. This assistant is to be chosen by O5-█ for loyalty to the Foundation, as well as psychological stability.

SCP-963 is to be attached to the subject's forehead or the back of the subject's hand using a suitably strong epoxy. SCP-963-1 is now hung by a chain from subject's neck. 963-1 is not allowed to be hidden upon the subject's body. Any attempt to do so will be met with lethal force.
If the current D-level subject exceeds a thirty-day life span, they are to be executed and a new subject chosen to wear 963-1. By order of O5-█, any body SCP-963-1 is installed upon is given a stay of execution until it passes on of natural causes, or 963-1 is transferred to a new host.

ATTENTION: As of 12/13/█████ 963-1 is not allowed in proximity of any Euclid or Keter class humanoid SCPs. This directive is to be enforced lethally. Rescinded, O5-6, O5-8, O5-9

ATTENTION: As of Incident-239-b Clef-Kondraki, SCP-963-1 is not allowed at Site 17 without the express permission of three O5's. Violations are to be met with lethal force. Rescinded, O5-6, O5-8, O5-9

J. Poole : Agent of the Foundation

Description: SCP-963-1 is an ornate amulet approximately 15 centimeters in circumference made from white gold, with thirteen (13) ██k brilliant-cut diamonds surrounding a ██k oval-cut ruby in a starburst pattern. It was discovered in the personal effects of ██████ ███ who had been found dead by apparent suicide, surrounded by a number of supernaturally-related books. Our Agent in the area found that 963-1 was incapable of being damaged and brought it in according to protocol XLR-8R-██.

Dr. Jack Bright,1 a Junior Staff researcher of good standing, was assigned the responsibility of researching SCP-963-1's capabilities, and granted access to [REDACTED]. Later that year, SCP-076-2 broke containment (see document 076-2-19A), leading to [REDACTED] deaths and ██ casualties. Doctor Bright was transporting SCP-963-1 by hand past SCP-076-2's containment unit, and was among the first KIB (killed in breach). Approximately █ days later, D1-113, tasked to clear the area of rubble, discovered 963-1 among the wreckage and picked it up. An immediate, noticeable change came over D1-113. Interview follows.

Interview Log x██████, Date: ██–██–██████

██████: Could you please tell me your name?

D1-113: It's Jack Bright, you damn well know it is!

██████: I believe you are Tom Higly, working for us as part of your life sentence.

D1-113: Don't be ridiculous! I couldn't possibly be- (SCP-963-1 is removed at this time from D1-113's possession. A further MRI shows that D1-113 ceases all higher brain functions. 963-1 is returned, upon which brain function returns.)

████: Dr. Bright?

D1-113: What?

████: We appear to have a problem.

After much experimentation, it has been discovered that when any living anthropoid comes into direct skin contact with SCP-963-1, the mind of the subject is wiped, and that of Dr. Bright is projected from 963-1 onto the subject. It is known that memories native to Dr. Bright transfer from host to host.
If a subject maintains contact for thirty (30) days, their brain functions become a duplicate of the late Dr. Bright's. If 963-1 is removed after this time period, the subject retains an independent copy of the consciousness of Jack Bright.
Sanctions were put in place to prevent multiple instances of Dr. Bright from being created to prevent Dr. Bright from collaborating with himself, however it was found this was not necessary, as Doctor Bright has proven thoroughly dedicated to the Foundation and its cause.
Doctor Bright himself has performed extensive experimentation on SCP-963-1, with the expressed desire for release from it. Interviews with Doctor Bright indicate that ████████ killed himself in the process of empowering SCP-963-1, and was therefore never able to slave his own consciousness to the amulet. Doctor Bright hypothesizes that he accidentally activated 963-1's power by being killed, instead of killing himself as the original creator had done.

J. Poole : Agent of the Foundation

ADDENDUM 2

THE THINGS DR BRIGHT IS NOT ALLOWED TO DO AT THE FOUNDATION

1. Telling new researchers that you can tame SCP-682 with a rolled up newspaper and a tummy rub is right out.
2. No longer allowed to challenge Able to unwinnable games like tic-tac-toe. It was three weeks before Able conceded a draw.
3. SCP-018 is not to be taunted!
4. Giving 113 to Diogenes is just plain pointless.
5. Attempting to disprove 343, to 343, is a horrible idea. Agents are still studying the resulting paperweight, supposedly so heavy that 343 should not be able to lift it.
6. While it is true that "No one expects the SCP Inquisition!", that is only because there is no such thing.
7. Dr. Bright is not king of anywhere. Or queen.
8. SCP-963 is not to be used for recreational or procreational purposes.
9. Although it is entirely possible to use SCPs currently under control of the Foundation to create tentacle monsters, no.
   1. Not even if Dr. Palmer asks nicely.
10. There is no market for SCP brand pornography.
    1. No, not even in Germany.
11. Should not replace the buckshot in Dr. Clef's shotgun shells with any of the following: birdseed, confetti, cake sprinkles, sawdust, or glitter.
12. The Better Business Bureau is not the correct agency for dealing with containment failures from horrible eldritch artifacts sold by Marshall, Carter, and Dark.
13. Victims of SCP-217 are not toys.
    1. Nor are they to be used as props at a Steampunk Convention.
14. Dr. Bright is not allowed to bargain with personnel for their "souls."Not even if he can get them a good deal.

J. Poole : Agent of the Foundation

15. Don't let Dr. Bright get a sample of SCP-379. Let my laptop be the last victim.

16. Not allowed to go off my medication.

17. May not use any form of the word 'accident' as an excuse.

18. Violate the dress code, even on 'casual' Fridays.

>   1. No matter how many times you say please, Dr. Bright, we won't put any of the hats you've been asking about into the dress code.

19. If an SCP file says never to do something, it is not because we want to control your mind. Yes it is.

>   1. No, it's not, and Dr. Bright may not edit this document.

20. SCP-437 is not to be handed out as weaponry to unsuspecting new researchers.

21. [DATA REDACTED ON O5 REQUEST]. Not even for recreational use.

22. Not allowed to send Nigerian-esque spam email to the Church of the Broken God.

23. Not allowed to lead a Mobile Task Force against the UIU under any circumstances. without inviting Dr. Clef at all. In fact, just stay 500 feet away from any Mobile Task Force at all times.

24. Not allowed to end reports with lyrics from "The Fresh Prince of Bel-Air".

>   1. But is allowed to end with lyrics from the Safety Dance.
>   2. The interpretive dance routine, however, is forbidden until he gets lessons for the foreseeable future.

25. Dr. Bright is not allowed anywhere near a Renaissance Festival.

>   1. Especially not with D-class in garb.

26. SCP-963 is not a joy buzzer.

27. If a mind-controlling SCP is discovered, it is to be turned

over to the proper authorities. It is not to be used to advance himself or others higher in the Foundation. Kondraki

28. Dr. Bright is NOT: A superhero of any sort, Head of Public Relations, in charge of Orientation for new staff, a doctor of psychology, a member of Site Command, made out of bacon, in possession of a IQ over 300, Head of SCP Review, or a member of Maintenance Staff. (Sorry boys, Dr. Bright IS a member of Site Command. It's usually best not to ask why. It's O5 Command you're thinking of.)

29. There is no Ethics Committee.
>1. And even if there was, does anyone believe Dr. Bright would be on it?
>2. As anything other than a 'What not to do?'

30. No longer allowed to make up jodies for morning calisthenics.
>1. Yes, this includes The Mickey Mouse Club song.

31. Dr. Bright is not allowed to apply SCP-963 to any major political figures. Again.

32. Dr. Bright is not from an alternate timeline.
>1. Dr. Bright cannot issue orders to "preserve the timeline".
>2. Or to "corrupt the timeline".
>3. Or to "screw with those history nerds".

33. Dr. Bright is not allowed to challenge anyone to a duel, and then give them SCP-572.

34. Dr. Bright is not allowed near SCP-5555-J in any way or any excuse. Remember what the miniature version did to Dr. L█████.

35. Dr. Clef and Dr. Bright are not allowed to interact without the presence of a responsible administrator.
>1. Dr. Kondraki does not count as a responsible administrator.
>2. Nor does Agent Strelnikov.
>3. Or Dr. Mann.
>4. In fact, let's just keep the two of them apart,

J. Poole : Agent of the Foundation
period.

36. Chainsaws are not the solution to every question.
    1. Nor is 'More Chainsaws'.
    2. Or "Chainsaw cannons"
    1. Except for that one time. And yes,
    it was awesome.

37. SCP speed dating never happened. Any one who claims to remember such an event should report to Site Command for administration of Class A amnesiac.

38. Dr. Bright is not allowed to use any SCP to alter or affect the outcomes of any reality based television shows, including but not limited to Survivor, Big Brother, Hell's Kitchen, American Idol, or any dating show on VH1.
    1. Not even if Dr. Rights asks nicely.

39. Dr. Bright is not allowed to administer spankings to Dr. Rights as punishment, as it only causes more rules to be broken.
    1. No, it doesn't matter that they are both "consenting adults", no matter how much either of them argue otherwise.
    2. Dr. Rights is not allowed to spank the monkey.
    3. Nor is she allowed to shock the monkey.
    4. Or anything else related to the monkey.

40. SCP-082 is not to be given song requests, especially not "Like A Virgin".

41. "Accidentally" spilling green gelatin on a dead body in the presence of the O5 was funny exactly once, and the smell of excrement exuding from O5-2's khakis spoiled the moment.

42. Dr. Bright is no longer allowed to utter the phrase "More than 1,000 babies" in the presence of any SCP personnel.

43. Nothing in the Foundation is rated 'Over 9000.'

44. Stop posting classified information on 4-chan.

45. No using SCP-705 for personal gain.
    1. Or to plant monitoring equipment.
    2. And absolutely no giving them tons of extra Play-Doh 'just to see what they can make.' That Mecha was

damned annoying!

46. If it involves doing something wrong, it isn't right.

47. If it involves something right, you did it wrong.

48. If Dr. Bright has to ask, it's above his clearance level.

> 1. If it's above Bright's security clearance… run.

49. Dr. Bright is not allowed to declare war on any country, thing or person.

50. Foundation credit cards or expense accounts are not to be used to purchase pornography.

> 1. Not even anomalous pornography.

51. Dr. Bright is not a "marital aid" and cannot refer to himself as such. Especially on official documents.

52. Dr. Bright is not the Lord of Rodly Might.

> 1. And is hereby banned from playing Dungeons and Dragons making use of SCPs to 'simulate the real danger.'

53. Dr. Bright is not allowed to go to fan conventions.

> 1. Let alone use them as recruitment drives.
> 2. Especially not at Furry Conventions.

54. When writing a report, more detail is expected than "Object class: Keter. Special Containment Procedures: [DATA EXPUNGED]. Description: [DATA EXPUNGED]."

> 1. And inventing new security clearances just so nobody can see what you've written is also considered poor form.

55. Showing Monty Python episodes to SCP-239 was not a wise decision. Please never try this with any other reality warping SCP.

56. "For the Emperor" is not an acceptable justification for any decision.

57. "My evil twin did it" is no longer considered a viable excuse.

> 1. Nor is "My good twin did it," considering the implications.

58. Yes, forum trolls are annoying. No, they don't automatically become D-class personnel.

59. Not allowed to lace 'orgasm muffins' with Ex-lax. Again.

60. Dr. Bright is not allowed to send e-mails with memetic

J. Poole : Agent of the Foundation
hazards attached.

    1. Not even when replying to spam.

61. The "Ultimate Showdown of Ultimate Destiny" is not grounds to pit more than fifteen combative SCPs, including SCP-682 and Able, against each other.

    1. "Weeding out some of these angsty teens with attitude problems," however, is.

    2. Dr. Bright is not allowed to administer 'Free Hugs.'

62. Not allowed to kick SCP-2558-J.

    1. Not allowed to play dodgeball with SCP-2558-J Not allowed to play any type of ball game with SCP-2558-J.

63. Any proposal which includes the phrase 'Metric Fuck Load' is straight out denied.

64. Instances of SCP-2558-J-Ex are not to be spooked when being held by members of O5. No instances of SCP-2558-J should be anywhere near an O5, let alone SCP-2558-J-Ex.

65. The Foundation motto is "Secure, Contain, Protect", not any of the following:

    1. "Stab Carrion Powerfully"

    2. "Let's use it on 682!"

    3. "Throw the cheese!"

    4. "That's it, you're on Keter Duty."

    5. "Can we put it in 914?"

    6. "Blood makes the grass grow, kill, kill, kill!"

    7. "Fuck trees, I climb clouds motherfucker!"

    8. "Someone is getting stabbed."

    1. But some days, it should be.

    9. "Whose hand is that?"

    10. "If all else fails, poop on it."

    11. "If all else fails, there's always the sun."

    12. "We need bigger kittens."

    13. "Society of Creepy Perverts."

    14. "Fuck Death, War, Famine and Pestilence. We've got Clef, Gears, Kondraki and Bright."

    15. "Throw D-Class at it until it stops."

16. "447 and dead bodies, two great tastes that taste great together."
17. "The FBI are a bunch of pansies."
18. "Who wants to see what I can make the president do in public?"
19. "For the Horde!"
20. "Science for the Science God!"
21. "Make sure to wipe your feet on 2558!"
22. "When in doubt, feed it to 682."
23. "Slapstick, Clowns and Puns"
24. "Drop the blanket now!"
25. "Seduction, Coitus, and Pregnancy"
26. "We always need more Dakka!"
27. "Still Alive, and Found the Cake"
28. "Don't Worry, O5 won't ever figure it out!"
29. "Will it blend?"
30. "Commies love us!"
31. "Snap Crackle and Pop"

66. Dr. Bright is no longer allowed to play "Hippocratic Oath Chicken" with the medical staff.

67. A full minute of stunned silence means "My God what did you do?" not "Please continue."

68. Pranks placed into new staff's desks are not funny because they "liquefied in record time."

69. Attempts to use Foundation radio telescopes to contact omniscient and omnipotent extraterrestrial entities will result in a bill for any damage to local space-time, including the cost of demoting objects to dwarf planet status.

70. Despite his doctoral degree, Dr. Bright is not allowed to either prescribe or administer any of the following:

1. enemas
2. homeopathic remedies
3. any sort of medication
4. free hugs
5. the healing power of laughter
6. sexual healing

J. Poole : Agent of the Foundation
7. 'more cowbell'

71. Dr. Bright is no longer allowed to offer the solution of "Use more guns" to any problem.

1. Or "Get bigger guns."

72. Despite what he may say and any evidence, no matter how plausible, the SCP Foundation has never and will never be associated with Hogwarts School of Witchcraft and Wizardry, and regardless of what Dr. Bright may say, he is not, and I quote, "A real life wizarding tutor."

1. Nor is he a vampire. That was body glitter and bad acting.
2. And despite what the computer file on him may say, he is not Muad'dib. The spice can flow just fine without him.

73. The "Tamlin House School of Witchcraft and Wizardry" is just a plain bad idea.

74. Yes, empirical evidence is the foundation of science. Yes, blind faith is the death of reason. No, this does not logically imply that anyone is ethically obligated to demonstrate the existence of breasts under laboratory conditions.

75. If Dr. Bright is ever found under the influence of any recreational substance, he must immediately be contained under level 15 containment. If you want to know why, please refer to the security tapes for ███ / █ / ███ between the hours of ██ : ██ am and ██ : ██ pm.

1. If Dr. Bright is found deliberately getting high to get out of paperwork, he is to be placed in a Type 4 cell and hosed down with cold water from a pressurised hose for no less than 5 minutes. Maybe this will teach you that drugs are bad, m'kay?

76. Cthulhu and R'lyeh are not valid reasons to send Pandora's Box out into the Pacific Ocean in order to capture them. Furthermore, these are not even SCPs, and I will find the person who decided to enter a database file for them.

77. Dr. Bright is not allowed to upload visual memetic kill

agents to 4chan 7chan any imageboard.

> 1. Well, okay, maybe to 4chan. It'd be doing the gene pool a service.

78. Dr. Bright cannot change the standard issue D-Class uniform to black pants with a red polo shirt.

> 1. I see your reasoning, but we just don't want to be associated with Star Trek.

79. No matter how many times he may claim it, no matter how many uniforms we may confiscate, Dr. Bright is not a ninja, nor has he ever been.

> 1. No. Not even if he uses SCP-281 to do it.

80. There are no security codes for:

> 1. Zombie conga line
> 2. Badass hat
> 3. Vampire can-can
> 4. Disco corpse
> 5. Intense homoeroticism
> 6. Extreme crotch violence
> 7. Man disguised as a palm tree
> 8. Man with porn 'stache
> 9. Kung fu rasta
> 10. Puppy-eating monks
> 11. Justifiable homicide of all you dumb ass mother humpers.
> 12. Bright Family Reunion (Code Brown. Find a place to hide, and make sure you leave an offering of booze outside your door.)
> 13. Dr. Kondraki beach party.

81. Just because Bright is a doctor does not mean that he is the Doctor, no matter how many British men he possesses.

> 1. No, SCP-963 is not proof against this.
> 2. Nor is any structure that results from placing SCP-184 inside of a police call box.
> 3. Adopting female members of the staff and calling them "companions" is right out.

> 4. SCP-297 is NOT a sonic screwdriver.
> 5. The Doctor who?

82. While humour can be an effective way to improve staff morale, it is highly inappropriate to make "Your mum" jokes in the vicinity of SCP-597.

83. Dr. Bright may not classify any researcher, including himself, as a memetic hazard.

84. Dr. Bright is no longer allowed to accept or use the following as payment for bets:

> 1. Your soul
> 2. Anyone else's soul
> 3. Virgin's blood
> 4. Reproductive organs
> 5. SCPs
> 6. Memories (real or imagined)
> 7. Pieces of your past I have no idea how that worked with Clef, but apparently he can do it.
> 8. The island of Manhattan
> 9. Beads
> 10. Firstborn children
> 11. Second-born children
> 12. Red-headed stepchildren
> 13. Rented mules
> 14. Gold spun from straw
> 15. A child's laughter
> 16. A child's tears
> 17. Virginity
> 18. Ponies
> 19. Anyone's grandmother
> 20. Anyone's grandfather
> 21. Anyone's sister
> 22. Any blood relative

85. No matter how many times he photoshops himself into a picture of SCP-682, and no matter how many Australians he possesses, Bright is not, and never was, the "Crocodile

Hunter".

      1. Nor does every SCP/D-Class "really hate it when you jam your thumb up their bum."

      1. And he is not allowed to do that "Right naow!"

86. As funny as Incident 387/682-█ was, Dr. Bright is not allowed unsupervised access to SCP-387. Researchers are still trying to figure out how an animate model of 682 was so invulnerable, despite only being made of just plastic blocks.

87. Dr. Bright is not allowed to tell new researchers experimenting on SCP-168 to divide by zero, find the square root of negative one, or find the last digit of pi using the SCP. Dr. █████████ is still comatose, and 168 itself is quite displeased with the event.

88. Dr. Bright is not allowed to use examples from Star Trek when administering Turing tests to artificial intelligences of any sort. Computer hardware does not grow on trees, dammit!

89. Dr. Bright is not allowed to plant SCP-2383-J into science labs. We're still picking up complaints from the office of Stephen Hawking.

      1. No, not even for the good of "SCIENCE"

      2. Or even as "Science for the Science God". Dr. Bright is also not allowed to refer to himself as such either.

90. Dr. Bright is not allowed to use SCP-587 to re-enact the locker scene from Men In Black, nor play Godzilla with its inhabitants.

      1. Nor is he allowed to set himself up as a god to them.

      2. Testing between SCP-786 and SCP-587 is also banned. "David and Goliath" scenarios are just as harmful to its inhabitants as the Godzilla incident.

      3. Dr. Bright is not allowed to use SCP-786 to simulate "Dwarf Fortress".

91. Dr. Bright is not allowed to show SCP-682 any of the

following:

      1. any Uwe Boll movies
      2. The Room
      3. Troll 2
      4. Manos: The Hands of Fate
      5. movies considered "so bad they're good"
      6. movies considered "cult classics"
      7. you know what, Dr. Bright is just not allowed to show SCP-682 any movies at all, ever.

92. Dr. Bright is not allowed to claim SCP-014-J has "Breached Containment" and then leave a dining fork in the hallway.

93. Dr. Bright is not O5-█-J. No such position exists at this time.

94. Dr. Bright is not allowed to give SCP-239 a copy of any Harry Potter books.
      1. What did you do?

95. Dr. Bright is not allowed to use SCP-141 to give people parking tickets.

96. Dr. Bright is not allowed to send anything into the past, future, or to alternate dimensions.

97. Dr. Bright is not allowed to accuse people of being duplicates of himself with the intention of having them terminated, unless they actually are duplicates of himself.
      1. Dr. Clef is not allowed to convince people Dr. Bright is a copy of him.

98. Dr. Bright may not put "A cup of orgasm" from SCP-294 through SCP-914 on the Very Fine setting.
      1. Dr. Bright may not use SCP-294 to create a "cup of memetic orgasm" and use it on worldwide television.
      2. Dr. Bright is not permitted to use SCP-294 to create orgasms of any kind, memetic, sentient or otherwise.
      3. Given the results of requesting a cup of "Dear

God No", Dr. Bright is no longer allowed to use SCP- 294 directly or outside of approved testing.

4. Given that he asked another staff member to request a "Cup of Explodium" from SCP-294 to "see what would happen", Dr. Bright is not allowed to ask other staff members to access SCPs for him, no matter how instructive, funny or helpful the results would be. The only exception to this is SCP-963.

99. Dr. Bright is not allowed to make, accept, or take a rake-off on, bets concerning XK-class End-of-the-World Scenarios.

100. Dr. Bright is no longer allowed access to SCP-732 infected documents along with SCP-239. MTF-Lambda-2 has been dispatched to contain "Chowderclef".

101. Dr. Bright is not allowed to organize, authorize, or create in any form, a "Foundation Demolition Derby, starring SCPs 2383-J, 708, 666-J, 2558-J, 1543-J, 2041-J, 2103-J, 968, 462, 115, and 225 for the grand finale" No.. just no. Not even if you try to throw in 682 trying to disguise it as a termination attempt.

102. Dr. Bright is not allowed to get on the PA system at site 19 and announce that he just won The Game You know what, Dr. Bright is just never allowed on the PA system for any reason, ever.

103. Dr. Bright is not allowed to request access to all cubical SCPs to make a fort of any kind.

104. Dr. Bright is not allowed to play "hot potato" with SCP-963.

105. Dr. Bright is not allowed to arrange, schedule, advertise, promote, or sell tickets to, "cage matches" between Able and SCP-682 any SCPs.

106. We don't care HOW many O5's agree to it and how many precedents there are, Dr Bright is not allowed a pet SCP.

107. Dr. Bright is not allowed to combine a cadaver infected

with SCP-008 with SCP-217.

108. Dr.'s Bright and Clef are no longer allowed to engage in ~~research~~ any activity involving ~~40 gallons~~ more than a pound any amount of superballs.

> 1. Also, the aforementioned are not to ~~convince~~ ~~blackmail~~ compel D-Class personnel anybody into conducting such activities for them.

109. "Challenge Accepted" is not a valid excuse for anything.

110. Dr Bright is not allowed to lease out SCP-002, even especially if he includes the option to buy.

111. Dr. Bright is not allowed to dress up as Joseph Stalin and ambush Agent Strelnikov in the hallways.

> 1. Actually, Dr. Bright shouldn't be allowed to dress up as any Communist dictator, there's no way it could end well.

112. Dr. Bright is not to be allowed access to the cafeteria menu more than ~~a day in advance~~ six hours in advance at all, nor is he to get anyone else to access it for him, directly or indirectly.

113. Dr. Bright is not allowed to introduce small children to the "the Giving Tree."

114. Dr. Bright is not allowed to 'borrow' SCP-159 for his office.

115. Dr. Bright is not allowed near any carbonated beverages while in possession of Mentos-branded mints. The last time that happened, he somehow managed to cause an earthquake in the East Coast of the United States. Dr. Bright is not allowed to claim responsibility for earthquakes and other natural disasters unless he is actually responsible for them.

116. Dr. Bright is not allowed to dare ~~new personnel~~ anyone to play 'peek-a-boo' with either SCP-569 or SCP-173.

117. When ordering things online, send them to PO Box █████ and not directly to Site 19. We've already had three postmen show up at the front door. (How did they even find

us?) Dr. Bright is not to give directions to Site 19 to non-Foundation personnel.

118. Dr. Bright is no longer allowed to give navigational directions to Site 19 anywhere, even especially to Foundation personnel.

119. The SCP Foundation does not have any such position as "Chief Defenestrator".

      1. Wrong.

      1. Agent Clef is not allowed to create new positions.

120. Any proposed containment procedure that includes the phrase "Giant Robot" is to be automatically rejected.

121. Excessive force is not the same as the Force, therefore using it does not make Dr. Bright a Jedi.

122. Dr. Bright is not allowed to use SCP-914 to craft items from Team Fortress 2.

      1. Yes, a Medigun would be a useful tool for the Foundation medical staff. No, we are not going to waste any more SCP-500 attempting to make one, especially not after SCP-427.

      2. Dr. Bright is not allowed to use SCP-914 to craft items from Minecraft, either. Also, your "Diamond Pickaxe" has been confiscated.

123. Dr. Bright is not allowed to tell future hosts that "You are about to become very Bright".

      1. And he can't tell anyone that "Possession is nine-tenths of the law".

      2. Dr. Bright is not allowed to refer to D-class personnel as "extra lives".

124. Dr. Bright is not allowed to send SCP-1004 over an email message.

125. No matter the electricity savings, no product of SCP-158 is to be used for illumination.

126. SCP-001 is not Dr. Bright's penis.

      1. The hammer is not his penis.

2. Dr. Bright is not allowed to use his genitals for construction purposes.

127. Dr. Bright possesses the ability of consciousness transfer and the artifact SCP-963. He does not possess any of the following:

1. "laser" eyes.
2. "laser" nostrils.
3. "laser" [REDACTED].
4. a Green Red ANY Lantern Ring.
5. an "adamantium" skeleton.
6. Anduril.
7. Mjolnir.
8. a map leading to "ALL OF THE NAZI GOLD".
9. the "Ancient" medallion.
10. a copy of the Necronomicon.
1. A King James version of the Necronomicon.
11. cybernetic implants of any kind.
12. the "Dragonzord". I don't care how you did it, put it BACK.
13. the 7th Element of Harmony.
14. infallible "gaydar".
15. The philosophers stone. [Technically speaking...]
16. the touch.
17. the power.
18. the "secret"
19. telepathy.
20. telekinesis.
21. the original filming model of any fictional spacecraft.
22. 1337 H4x00r sKi11z.
23. the 6th sense.
24. The ability to distinguish between butter and I Can't Believe It's Not Butter.

128. If Dr. Bright's current form is sighted near an armory

without express permission, initiate Evacuation Procedure ████-██.

129. Dr. Bright is not allowed to test SCP-826 with his self-authored comic book entitled "Dr. Bright and the 79 Virgins" Playboy magazines anything.

130. #%^&@Dr. Bright iz a genius! Second best only to meh! he & I are buds lolz!#$%^

    1. Dr. Bright is not allowed to give SCP-732 access to this document.

        1. Dr. Bright is not allowed to give any SCP access to this document without O5 approval.

131. Dr. Bright is not allowed to tell new D-Class personnel that SCP-439 has escaped into the barracks.

132. Dr. Bright is not allowed to convince other personnel that they are actually Dr. Bright.

133. Dr. Bright is not allowed to challenge SCP-082 to a drinking contest. (Even if he's positive he can win.)

134. We have never had a Jamaican Vacation Giveaway, Dr. Bright is not in charge of it, and SCP-342 is not the official Foundation Travel Voucher.

135. Dr. Bright is not allowed access to SCP-243 except under strict supervision. I think we all remember the great marital-aid migration of 2011.

136. Dr. Bright is not allowed to challenge Dr. Gerald to a race involving any sort of vehicle. Dr. Bright is not allowed to challenge Dr. Gerald to a race involving anything.

137. Dr. Bright is not allowed to access the IT department hotline access the IT department database access any networking equipment belonging to the IT department.

138. Dr. Bright is not to bring samples of SCP-1361 to Foundation potlucks, barbeques, or charity food drives.

139. SCP-963 is not a 'soul gem', and making a contract with Dr. Bright will not turn you into a 'magical girl'.

        1. Not even if he includes a 'magical girl outfit'.

140. SCP-963 is not the Soul Gem. Bright does not have

access to the Infinity Gauntlet. Please stop glaring at people who annoy you and snapping.

141. SCP-137 is never to be used on sex toys.
> 1. Under no circumstances is Dr. Bright allowed to expose SCP-137 to Warhammer 40K minifigures. Again. Not even in an attempt to terminate SCP-682.
> 2. Or anything made by Wondertainment.

142. Not allowed to have Able get into arguments with forum trolls.

143. Dr. Bright is not allowed to go trick-or-treating, ever.

144. Able is not Kratos.

145. Dr. Bright is no longer allowed to produce, create or remind staff of "SCP Robot Wars".

146. Copies of SCP-1981 are not to be submitted to "America's Funniest Home Videos".
> 1. Or posted on YouTube.
> 2. Or on YouPorn.
> 3. Or to Tosh.0.

147. Dr. Bright is not allowed to "Just Say No!" to O5 orders on the grounds that they are instances of SCP-5200-J.

148. Dr. Bright is also not allowed to refer to O5 Command MTF commanders the Janitor any Foundation personnel as "the cool kids".

149. Dr. Bright is not the "final boss" of anything.

150. Dr. Bright has not "won the internet" and is not authorized to declare that any other individual has done so.
> 1. Nor is he allowed to claim or distribute instances of SCP-335 under said premise.

151. Dr. Bright is not to show junior staffers his 'cutie mark'.
> 1. Dr. Bright is not allowed to use SCP-137 on any Hasbro product.

152. Dr. Bright is not allowed to "take SCP-1187 for a morning ride".

153. Dr. Bright is not allowed to submit any incident reports to

the Darwin Awards. Not even if you are sure it would win.

154. Dr. Bright is not allowed to teach SCP-1370 to play multiplayer video games. It was not an improvement giving it the vocabulary of the average preteen ███ player, or introducing it to the concept of "teabagging."

155. The eye-pods do not need hats, bow ties or any other form of clothing.

156. Dr. Bright is not allowed to use expunged data in SCP reports as "mad-libs."

157. Robo-Dude is not a piece of the Broken God.

158. Dr. Bright is not allowed to create an anatomically-correct body pillow modeled after SCP-173, SCP-105, SCP-076-02, or Dr. Crow.

159. The following are not appropriate sources for D-class personnel:

> 1. Temp agencies.
> 2. Craigslist.
> 3. Reality show talent pools.
> 4. Jerry Springer tapings.
> 5. "Orphans."
> 6. "Urchins."
> 7. "Ragamuffins."
> 8. "Those sons of bitches who scratched up my paint job at the car wash."
> 9. Ex-girlfriends.
> 10. Ex-boyfriends.
> 11. Ex-partners of any gender variation whatsoever.
> 12. Staff members' in-laws.
> 13. Youtube comment threads.
> 14. Forum trolls.
> 15. Angsty teens.
> 16. Bad applications to the SCP Foundation. Two exceptions have been made, but the rest are off limits.

J. Poole : Agent of the Foundation

17. Occupy Wall Street.
18. The Tea Party.
19. The Green Party.
20. The "Green" Party.
21. The Gathering of the Juggalos.
  1. How the fuck do they work?
160. The following items are not SCPs:
1. Rainbows.
2. Double rainbows.
3. "Rainbooms", whether sonic or otherwise.
4. The tides.
5. The Moon.
6. "Fucking magnets".
7. Rocks that skip three times before they go underwater.
8. Soy cheese.
9. Hippies.
10. Hipsters.
11. "MILFs."
12. "G-MILFs."
13. "GG-MILFs."
14. "Actually funny SNL skits" As these do not exist, they cannot be SCPs.
15. Anyone's breasts.
16. People who can solve Rubik's Cubes (of any size).
17. Shiny Any Pokemon.
161. Nobody ever refers to Dr. Bright as "Tim" and he is no longer allowed to introduce new personnel to SCP-524.
162. The platypus is not an SCP. No, really. No, not even an -EX.
163. Dr. Bright is not allowed to test internet "Creepypasta" rites using Class-D personal.
164. SCP-963 is not a "Millennium" item.
165. Dr. Bright should refrain from trying to convince SCP-

237 to become a "Brony".

> 1. Not even to improve his disposition.
>
> 2. For that matter, trying to make SCP-042 a Brony will just make things worse.

166. Putting an equine, no matter how small, through SCP-914 on very fine again is strictly forbidden.

> 1. No you cannot keep it.

167. The answer to a containment breach is never to "recruit a team of teenagers with attitude".

> 1. Or to "send five rings to five special young people".
>
> 2. Or to ask junior staffers if they are "bad enough dudes" to contain the breach.

168. Dr. Bright is not allowed to claim he "has been trained to conquer galaxies".

169. Dr. Bright may not attempt to neutralize SCP-682 using "the Power of Friendship", "the Power of Love", or any other sort of "Power" which has not been proven to actually exist.

170. Dr. Bright does not remind anyone of "the babe with the power of voodoo", and is not allowed to tell anyone else that they remind him of same.

171. The Chaos Insurgency has no interest in "summoning Daemons to the material universe to serve the Ruinous Powers of Chaos" and therefore, Dr. Bright is not permitted to inform new researchers otherwise.

172. Dr. Bright is not allowed to write a SCP-582 account in order to deal with junior staff members who get on his nerves.

173. Dr. Bright is not allowed to stick refrigerator magnets to Foundation equipment SCP-914 SCP-882 SCP-217 victims piece of the Broken God Any magnetic objects within Foundation control.

174. SCP-1916 only works if administered orally. We know this. There is no reason to test further, Dr. Bright.

175. "Why not?" is not considered authorization for SCP cross-testing.

176. The foundation has no Mobile Task Force dedicated to the capture and containment of forum trolls.

> 1. Dr. Bright is not allowed to found a new Mobile Task Force dedicated to the capture and containment of forum trolls.

177. The Serpent's Hand is not a synonym for masturbation.

178. "Yo mama" is not "so ugly SCP-096 didn't look at her."

179. SCP-173 is not a babysitter. Having SCP-173 play 'Where's the baby?' is downright cruel. Not, as Dr. Bright claims, '[EXPLETIVE] hilarious.'

180. Dr. Bright is no longer invited to the Annual Foundation Holiday Party.

> 1. Dr. Bright is not allowed to host his own Foundation Holiday Party.
> 2. The Foundation Holiday Party is cancelled indefinitely.

181. SCP-682 does not have a Wondertainment logo stamped on its upper palate.

> 1. or on its posterior.

182. Playing the song "Thriller" in the presence of SCP-008 victims is expressly forbidden.

> 1. Letting out SCP-008 victims and punching them "to simulate Minecraft" is also forbidden.
> 2. Pushing several agents in front of SCP-008 victims "to simulate Resident Evil" is not a valid excuse, either.
> 3. Dr. Bright is no longer allowed near victims of SCP-008.

183. SCP-682 will not be sated by the ritual sacrifice of a virgin.

184. Filming, directing, or performing in celebrity sex tapes are not appropriate work assignments for Mr. Deeds.

185. Anything involving the words "elephant sauce". Site 19 is still recovering from the last incident.

186. "I like a little junk in the trunk" is not valid authorization to

feed SCP-1575-1 to an elephant.

187. Dr. Bright is, under no circumstances, to attempt possession of SCP-682.

188. "I touched SCP-1453 a lil' while ago" is not a valid excuse for any containment breach.

189. "No Shirt, No Shoes, No Service" does not imply that pants and undergarments are not required parts of the dress code.

> 1. Doubly so, since, "No Shirt, No Shoes, No Service," is not a part of any official foundation dress code.

190. Dr. Bright is not to use this list as a resume.

191. Dr. Bright ~~shalt not~~ may not begin his sentences with "Thou shalt not", even ~~especially~~ in the presence of SCP-343.

192. Use of ~~double~~ ~~triple~~ ~~quadruple~~ ANY number of negatives to obtain security clearances will result in the repetition of ~~kindergarten~~ swift punishment.

193. Dr. Bright is not allowed to recreate any experiment seen on the television program "Mythbusters" using any SCP.

> 1. Especially not if he "can do it better."

194. Regardless of whether or not it exists, Dr. Bright certainly does not enjoy diplomatic immunity as the local Consul of the Islamic Republic of Eastern Samothrace.

195. Dr. Bright is not allowed to put SCP-278 into SCP-914 on coarse "so I can learn to make more of them."

196. Dr. Bright is not allowed to ~~transfer~~ ~~copy~~ ~~upgrade~~ relocate SCP-079 onto ANY form of high capacity data storage device.

197. SCP-1156 is not Dr. Bright's "royal steed".

198. Dr Bright is not allowed to use SCP-1543-J to launch SCP-727-J into itself. Again.

199. Even if Dr. Bright is wearing an eyepatch, he is not allowed to "Keel-Haul" anyone.

> 1. Not even on "Talk Like a Pirate Day".
>
> 2. Talk Like a Pirate Day is not allowed to be

celebrated at Site ▆. Any personnel violating this rule will walk the plank be severely disciplined.

3. There is no such thing as "Talk Like a Ninja" day, and Dr. Bright is not allowed to create it.

200. Introducing SCP-682 to SCP-002 "just to see what will happen" is NOT recommended. Don't even think about.

1. I SAID STOP THINKING ABOUT IT!

201. Dr. Bright is no longer allowed to interview new personnel.

1. ~~Even~~ Especially not if they ask for him.

202. Dr. Bright is not Kenny. We also ask new researchers (and Bright) to stop referring to him/self as such.

203. Dr. Bright is not allowed to play "SCP Roulette" with SCP-173, a light switch and any combination of D-class and new personnel.

204. Dr. Bright is not to ask SCP-738, "What would you want in exchange for not making this deal with me?"

205. Dr. Bright works for the SCP Foundation, not the Terminus Foundation. He does not possess a degree in psychohistory.

1. And no Group of Interest is the "Second Foundation"

206. The fact that SCP-682 regenerates all lost tissue does not make it an "infinite hamburgers machine".

1. Most especially because they tasted horrible.

207. Dr Bright is not allowed to use SCP-127 to place projectiles under his pillow for the "Tooth Fairy" to give him money.

208. Dr Bright is not allowed to use SCP-252-ARC on ~~Fred Phelps~~ any member of the Phelps family any person or organization affiliated with Westboro Baptist Church.

1. Dr Bright is not allowed to attempt to "sic the Horizon Initiative" on the above religious organization.

    2. Dr Bright may not request a pool of D-Class recruited solely from members of the above religious organization.

209. The Manna Charitable Foundation does not host an annual Labor Day Telethon, and Dr. Bright is not allowed to offer the services of Foundation employees as performers or phone bank operators for such.

210. Dr Bright is not allowed access to Popular Science Magazine. That How 2.0 section is way too dangerous for Bright to see now that they've shown how to create cyborg cockroaches.

211. Dr. Bright is not allowed to "go on crusade".

    1. Or on "jihad".

    2. Dr. Bright is not permitted to issue fatwas against anyone or anything.

212. Dr. Bright is no longer allowed to declare "After ten thousand years I'm free! It's time to conquer Earth!" upon assuming a new host.

213. All Foundation personnel are now required to attend a seminar on the difference between an original idea and a good idea before being allowed new or continuing contact with Dr. Bright, Dr. Clef, or Dr. Kondraki.

214. Dr. Bright does not have ten tons of gold hidden somewhere at Site 19.

215. SCP-963 is not to be given away as a "good luck charm".

216. Dr. Bright is not a wizard, no matter what he might tell you.

    1. He is not an alchemist either, and is not to be consulted regarding alchemical issues.

    2. Or a witch.

    3. Dr. Bright is not magic and cannot perform magic, and must give sufficient explanation for any actions he undertakes.

217. Dr. Bright is not, nor has he ever been, the "Undisputed SCP Intercontinental Champion".

218. Dr. Bright is no longer allowed to run through Site 19 any site while screaming "THE KETER IS LOOSE" unless it's an actual emergency.

> 1. Claiming it's for research on the effects of social engineering is not an emergency.
> 2. Nor is using it to clear out the areas Dr. Bright is otherwise restricted from entering due to reasons given on this list.
> 3. Dr. Bright may not start referring to any persons or SCPs as "The Keter" in order to circumvent these rules, unless they are actually classified as Keter.

219. Dr. Bright is not allowed to perform any tests or experiments utilizing the reproductive organs of any dead or living being, including himself.

220. Dr Bright may not tell D-Class Personnel newly recruited staff anyone that SCP-920 will "show them to their quarters". Again. We are still looking for 12 D-class Personnel who have disappeared in the Pyrenees.

221. Dr. Bright may never attempt to ingest SCP-184 "to win a pie eating contest", nor any other kind of eating or drinking contest.

222. After what happened last month, Dr. Bright is not allowed to watch Firefly ever again. I think most of the people involved (that are still alive) are still in the psychiatric ward.

> 1. Dr. Bright is not a Brown Coat, and we CAN stop the signal.
> 2. Dr Bright IS a leaf on the wind, watch him so- Still too soon? Okay.

223. Dr. Bright is not allowed to come within 5 meters of any explosive device or detonation device. Remember what happened at Area-█.

> 1. Not even if Dr. Iceberg asks nicely
> 2. Trying to "Blow Up 682" is not a valid excuse.

224. Attempting to make "shadow puppets" with SCP-017 is

forbidden.

>1. Trying to entertain SCP-053 is not a valid excuse.

225. Dr. Bright is no longer allowed to stand in a corner and twiddle his thumbs.

226. Dr. Bright is no longer allowed to use the words "swag" , "swag it", "swagginator", "swaggify", or "super swag" to define himself or any other person(s).

227. 'YOLO' is not an excuse for anything. Most especially because it does not apply to him.

>1. Neither is 'Why not?'.

228. Dr. Bright is not allowed to order D-class personnel convince new personnel any personnel ask anybody ever to play a game of patty-cake with SCP-049.

229. Dr. Bright is not allowed to ask Mr. Deeds to do any of the things on this list.

230. Dr. Bright is not allowed to bring chocolate into a restroom Dr. Bright is not allowed to bring food into a restroom.

231. Dr. Bright is not allowed to speak in a voice resembling a movie character.

>1. Dr. Bright is not allowed to reenact any movie. Even G-rated ones? Even G-rated ones.

232. Dr. Bright is not allowed to learn cheerleader routines dress like a cheerleader do ANYTHING relating to the sport of cheerleading.

233. SCP-957 is NOT a prerequisite to becoming possessed by Dr. Bright

234. Dr. Bright is not allowed access to SCP-1197 for the purpose of corroborating with himself.

>1. Dr. Bright is not allowed access to SCP-1197 for the purpose of propositioning himself.

235. As of 9/26/20█, Dr. Bright is not allowed access to any hotel for any reason. Site-█ budget does not allow for extra clean-up fees, especially not as a result of Dr. Bright's actions.

236. Dr. Bright is no longer allowed to say "Everything the Bright touches is our kingdom"

237. Dr. Bright may not attempt to digitally enhance any of the original Star Wars movies.

238. Dr. Bright is not allowed to advertise himself on online dating services.

239. Dr. Bright is not allowed to use this list as a to-do list.

240. Dr. Bright is not L. Ron Hubbard incarnate, and is not allowed to tell personnel otherwise.

241. Dr. Bright is not Sherlock Holmes and is not allowed to say what he thinks a person's appearance means about them to any reality bending SCP.

> 1. Dr. Bright is not allowed to cause a containment breach of any kind just so he can have a "case."
>
> 2. Neither is he allowed to convince anyone to be Watson.

242. Dr. Bright may not urge bereaved staff members to "look at the Bright side".

> 1. Nor is he allowed to refer to any name-related puns as "[his] Bright ideas".
>
> 2. Dr. Bright is not allowed to refer to any SCPs, Foundation resources, or personnel as his "fancy dancing pants".

243. Dr. Bright is not allowed to use SCP-1994-J with Dr. Kain. Hours of actual productive research are as of yet to be recovered.

244. Dr. Bright is no longer allowed to play chicken with members of any department.

245. Dr. Bright is not allowed to order 'the works' from the cafeteria.

> 1. Dr. Bright is also not allowed to put anything on his 'tab.'

246. Dr. Bright is no longer allowed to commit "Seppuku."

> 1. Even if he has an audience.

2. Especially a captive one.

247. Dr. Bright is not in possession of any of the following: A bright-mobile, brighterangs, a bright-claw, a bright-suit, or a baseball-bright.

      1. Dr. Bright is not allowed to yell "To the brightcave!".

248. Dr. Bright is no longer allowed to sing "Silent Night" following the "All is Bright" incident

249. Dr. Bright is no longer allowed to commission, produce, advertise, or display animated videos to containment
staff anyone with the subject, "What Happens When You Fuck Up Containing SCP (insert SCP here)"

      1. NO, it is NOT educational, Bright. Not the way you show it.

250. Dr. Bright is not allowed funding to replicate the experiments of Doctor Krieger from Archer.

251. Dr. Bright is not allowed to try to convince personnel to replicate "his famous high dive into SCP-120."

      1. He is not allowed to talk about his "famous high dive into SCP-120."

252. Dr. Bright is not to be referred to as "Rainbow Bright".

253. Dr. Bright is not allowed access to infants for the purpose of becoming "the Baby New Year".

254. Dr. Bright is not allowed to create a "The Things Dr Bright Is Allowed To Do At The Foundation" list by listing everything that isn't on this list. Just because it isn't on this list doesn't mean you should do it.

      1. He may however request for one to be created.

      2. He may not, however, suggest what should be on said list.

255. Dr. Bright is not to attempt to neutralize SCP-1013 just because he "can do Fluttershy's stare."

256. Dr. Bright must not create an infinite logical loop to less feeble minded individuals.

257. There is no such department known as "The Bright Ideas Department." Furthermore, if such a department did exist, Dr. Bright would not be in the employ of this department.

258. Dr. Bright is not allowed to throw himself through a window "to prove that the glass is unbreakable." for any reason whatsoever.

259. Dr. Bright is not allowed to convince D-Class anybody to cough in front of SCP-049

260. Dr. Bright is not allowed to use any green dyes for the purpose of "being creative".

261. "Because reasons" will no longer be accepted as a viable excuse for removing ANY SCP from containment.

262. Dr. Bright may not refer to anyone as a "peasant."

263. Dr. Bright is not allowed to attempt to convince D-Class new personnel ANYONE that shouting "Bing bong, bring it on!" while ringing SCP-513 will negate its effect.

264. Dr. Bright is not allowed to arrange gladiatorial arena combat between D-class, even ESPECIALLY if any SCPs are used as weapons.

265. SCP-173 does not "just want a hug" and Dr. Bright may not attempt to convince anyone otherwise.

266. "Because there's an alternate universe me who wouldn't do it" is no longer a valid reason for violating containment procedures.

267. Dr. Bright is not allowed to attack instances of SCP-217 claiming that "the Borg have attacked".

268. Dr. Bright is not allowed access to visual or audio recordings of the dance craze dubbed the "Harlem Shake" anything deemed "viral".

269. Dr. Bright is not allowed to start any drag races between D-classes in cars and SCP-096.

270. Dr. Bright is not allowed to yell out "Immigration!" near any foreign personnel.

271. Dr. Bright is not allowed to reenact any scene from "Pulp Fiction".

272. Doctor Bright is not allowed to convince new personnel ANYONE to "have a friendly staring contest with SCP-096."

273. Dr. Bright is not allowed to open SCP-1025 on random pages in front of anyone.

274. Dr. Bright is not allowed to dare anyone to finish SCP-1997.

275. Dr. Bright is not allowed to send a Slinky down SCP-087.

276. Dr. Bright is not an instance of SCP-1000, and is not allowed to claim otherwise.

    1. Especially not when using the body of a primate.

277. Dr. Bright is not allowed to use SCP-884 for shaving purposes.

    1. Nor any other personal care purpose.

    2. Nor for any non-approved purpose whatsoever.

    3. Especially not for the purpose of making people doubt that he's not allowed to use it.

278. Dr. Bright is not allowed to claim that Researcher Zyn Kiryu is the new "Master of Butterflies" due to her extensive work on butterfly-related SCP items.

    1. "King of the Booterflies" is not an inheritable title. No, not even if Kondraki really is dead, which, if true, Dr. Bright isn't cleared to know.

    2. Researcher Zyn Kiryu is also not to be referred to by Dr. Bright as "Queen of the Butterflies", "Mistress of the Butterflies", "Supreme Princess of the Butterflies", "Great Shepherd of the Butterflies", "Second Cousin of the Butterflies", or "Major Associate of the Butterflies

279. Dr. Bright is not allowed to tell new Foundation recruits fictional horror stories involving his family.

280. Dr. Bright is not allowed to tell new Foundation

recruits factual horror stories involving his family.

281. He is definitely not allowed to edit the list just to mess with people on Tumblr.

282. We do not talk about Bottle Dick.

> 1. Especially not over the site intercom/loud speaker/mega phone/group chat/email, or any other device intended to speak to large numbers of people at the same time.

283. We really mean it about editing the List to mess with people on Tumblr.

284. Dr. Bright is not allowed to transfer his consciousness into a YouTuber in order to make serious videos about himself or his family.

> 1. ESPECIALLY if it's all true.

285. Okay, who thought it was a good idea to let him have a tiktok account to read off all of these? @capnduckman on TikTok.

286. Dr. Bright is not Hades, nor any other greek god.

> 1. I don't care of it's Hercucles version or Lore Olympus, wash off the blue body paint, NOW.

> 2. And please stop trying to set your hair on fire.

287. There are NO plans to shut down any site to prevent Corvid-19 infection

> 1. That being said, if certain staffers do not start WASHING THEIR GODAMN HANDS after using the bathroom, Dr. Bright has full permission to be himself at them. I'm looking at you Magnus.

Steven L. Stamm

THE END OF BOOK 1

BOOK 2 COMING FEBRUARY 14TH 2021

Printed in Great Britain
by Amazon